the apologetic and yummy-looking Officer Cole lean against the kitchen wall. "I'm sorry about not coming to follow up. I talked to New York. Your stalker is quite persistent from the report. I also know that the identity is unknown."

Charly was sure she had mentioned this all last night. Right. Cute, confused, and deaf. How quickly she forgot.

"Yes." She poured the coffees, added sugar to his, stirred, and passed it to him.

"Thanks."

"You're welcome." She turned back to her mug and proceeded to the fridge where she hauled out the flavored creamer before she returned over to her mug. "So, you wanted to apologize."

"Yeah, I'm sorry. Actually, I think we should sit down over dinner and discuss what we can do to ensure you and your daughter's safety."

Having finished stirring the creamer into her mug, she turned and blinked at him in disbelief as she placed the spoon down and picked up the mug. "Now you want me to cook you dinner?"

He smiled. Okay, yeah, he was cute. "Not exactly, Charly."

**Dear Reader,**

Thank you   for purchasing *Sinfully Yours.* This book was originally released in 2007 as *Raining Men.* I thought the premise would be light hearted and fun. What woman wouldn't want three gorgeous men perusing her?

I really hope you enjoy Charly's story and the misadventures of love, art and having crazy friends.

~Best,

JT
www.jtschultz.com

# Sinfully Yours

By
JT Schultz

*Thank you*
*JT Schultz*

**SINFULLY YOURS**
Copyright © 2014 JT Schultz
Cover Art by JT Schultz © 2014
Edited by Bireanna Denton 2014 – No
Copyright Assigned

Second Edition 2014
ISBN-13: 978-1503094246

# Dedication

To my readers, thank you for the love and support over the years. To my new and first time readers, welcome to my crazy.

# Chapter One

"Charly! My God, think about it. You need to get laid in the worst way," Charlene Jamieson's friend Liz stated through the telephone receiver.

"Liz, I don't need sex." She scanned the room, wondering where she had left her coffee. "I own a fantastic vibrator and don't have to explain the naked men I see on a regular basis to the battery operated device. I simply turn it off and shove it in my drawer next to my thongs."

A snort came from the other end of the receiver. "Charly, let's clarify. You paint and take pictures of men. You don't do anything else with them. Next, you put all your lustful thoughts into your artwork. Have you thought maybe it would be more fun to put them into a man?" Liz chuckled sinfully. "Or have him put a whole lot of lust into you, repeatedly, until you climax and, with a little luck, see stars from the intensity?"

Charly sighed. This wasn't what she needed to hear or be discussing. Her new house still was in boxes from the move and her gallery opening was in just over three weeks. She was busy with her career and with her eight-year-old, Leigh. "I don't have time for a man."

*And less time for a conversation on how I need*

*a man. I do need to find my coffee cup, though.*

"Don't have time? For Christ's sake, Charly, you have them naked already. It's not rocket science. It's good, old-fashioned, body sweating, primal grunting, head thrown back as a climax seizes your soul kind of sex." She paused. "You do remember what that is, right?"

Ten sarcastic remarks filtered through her mind and she decided against all of them in case they did was fuel Liz and the conversation forward into more details about Liz's sex life than Charly wanted. Finally, she sighed and decided to answer her old high school friend. "Yes, I remember what sex is."

"Oh! That reminds me, has Officer Skippy stopped by yet for your safety check?"

*Wow, subject change out of nowhere. Oh well, I should be thankful we are no longer discussing my sex life…or hers.*

"No, I have absolutely no idea why the police in New York contacted someone here. Moreover, for someone who usually handles stalking cases, I've been here two weeks and nothing. I haven't even gotten an email from the illustrious, not to mention, failing at his job—Officer Cole Scepetti."

Liz and their other friend Jenna had nicknamed him Skippy. It was simply because the guy was apparently as smart as a peanut and just as useless.

"Maybe the officer will be as hot as hell

and can help with your crazy fan by guarding you from on top of you in bed."

"And you're back to my lack of sex life."

Liz giggled then sighed. "You're right, I'm sorry." Another laughed escaped her friend. "It doesn't have to be over you in bed. Hell, if he's hot, he can bend you over the table or the sofa. Hell, honey, if he's hot, just take his protection to the hilt."

Not even pausing to find out or debate if Liz meant sexual connotation, Charly sighed and wished the conversation could be switched to something like...well... Anything. "I doubt he's good-looking. He's probably old, fat, and can only bring his car to a stop for old ladies, small furry animals, including squirrels, and doughnuts."

"Oh hell, listen honey, one of my clients is calling. I have to call you back."

"Okay." Charly hung up the phone, relieved that, for the time being, her friend wasn't available for another lecture about Charly's social life. She glanced around the room and discovered the coffee mug sitting on the mantle of the fireplace. She had no idea how it had gotten there, or why she would even set it there, but on the bright side, she located the item containing undoubtedly cold coffee.

She reached for her mug and walked into the kitchen where the debate to pour it out and get fresh or just heat it in the microwave took place. It wasn't a life-changing decision, but today, the minor act seemed to dictate her fate. She voted for dumping the liquid. The thought of reheated coffee was as appealing as leftovers from a meal you didn't enjoy the first time.

Charly stepped over to the sink, dumped out her coffee, then leaned over to the coffee pot and poured a fresh one. Her doorbell sounded. Some days, she had no luck, and depending who was at the door, another cup of coffee was going to die freezing to death, then get tossed over the metal cliff known as the sink to the lower level of hell, which, in truth, was the drain.

She set the coffee with the low survival rate on the counter and walked to the door. Charly looked out the window from between the closed blinds and saw a strange man. Her stomach lurched to her throat and memories of her obsessed and stalker fan plagued her. She had moved her daughter and herself life from New York back to California because some fan wouldn't leave her alone. It was scary, considering that she had no idea what said fan she was running from looked like.

She whimpered and sounded like a scared kitten.

*Bravery at its best.*

Shooting a glance to the locked door, she

was thankful she had remembered to flip the bolt after Leigh left for school that morning. The doorbell went again, and Charly's heart picked up speed. She needed a weapon, and looked to the stove where the wooden block held a sharp knife set.

She scooted over to it in an ungraceful, cowardly shuffle, and grabbed the first knife she could. It was a steak knife. Not the biggest knife, but it wasn't the size that mattered; it was how it was used. With the knife concealed behind her back and newfound courage, she undid the bolt and opened the door. She smiled in a way that undoubtedly resembled serial killer. "Hello?"

The young man on the step smiled and revealed a mouthful of metal. She was stunned and slightly confused. Weren't braces clear these days? If only they were when she'd been in middle school. She probably would have had more confidence.

"Charlene Josephine Jamieson?"

Charly's heart hit the grey-flecked tile in her front entrance that desperately needed to be mopped. She clutched the knife tightly behind her back, knowing that she was prepared to use it without hesitation since she had to mop anyways. "Who wants to know?"

The young possible assailant she would kill in a heartbeat raised his brows and widened his eyes in what looked like... fear?

"Always Safe Alarm Company."

After releasing the breath she didn't realize she'd been holding, she smiled. "Oh, thank heavens." She pulled open the door further. "Please, come in." She waved with her other hand. His face turned ashen as his eyes fixed on the knife.

*Oh yeah, it's going to be one of those days.*

She laughed nervously. Quickly, she pulled the knife back behind her, resumed serial killer position, and smiled. "Sorry, I can't be too careful."

Brace-face nodded once and smiled like one would before throwing up after a roller coaster ride. "Right." He didn't sound convinced, but stepped into the house.

Charly shut the door behind him as he turned and watched her lock the door again. He glanced in the direction of where the knife was and looked terrified. As long as he didn't wet himself, she would be okay. She wondered silently what the difference between the blood and his liquid fear would be.

She backed away slowly, since she had already scared the life out of him. She wasn't in the mood to get the mop bucket yet. "So, are you here to put my alarm in?"

He nodded and glanced at the knife. "Not that you really need one."

*Funny joke. It was a joke, right?*

She smiled weakly. Maybe she had

overreacted a notch. In truth, it was a little drastic. "Go ahead and do your thing. I'll let color return to your face and permit your heart to start beating again by putting the knife away."

"I would be grateful." His eyes ran down her legs, and a devious smile came to his lips.

The doorbell went again. "Excuse me." She moved to the door.

He turned and cast a skeptical expression. "Can I recommend putting the knife down first?"

Charly smiled. The man had a point. She set the knife on the counter and peeked out the window to see the elderly woman who lived directly across from her. She opened the door. "Hello?"

"God bless, child. I'm Mrs. Newman, your neighbor. I thought I would come over with some brownies and a message from God. Do you know how much Jesus loves you?"

Her brows lifted in shock. *Oh, hell.* Why had she been convinced to put the knife down? "Hi, Mrs. Newman, please come in."

The neighbor stepped into the house, allowing Charly to shut the door. The phone rang. "Excuse me, Mrs. Newman." She headed to the phone in the living room. "Hello?" she greeted as she picked the cordless off the charger.

"Are you getting lucky yet?" Liz asked

from the other end of the line. "Hell, in that neighborhood, you should be getting laid every five minutes." Liz laughed. "I got rid of the client whose wedding I don't want to plan and thought I would call you back. That way, we can talk more about you needing a real flesh-and-blood man between your legs instead of one that is battery dependent. Can you talk? "

*Talk? Oh yeah, sure, let me get the church lady and alarm dude comfortable and pass out refreshments.*

Charly sighed and smiled at Mrs. Newman, who had followed her into the living room. She was currently eyeing the dork from the alarm company. "No, actually, I can't."

"So, are you the boyfriend?" Mrs. Newman asked the alarm dude.

*How can she really think he's my type? What is my type? I don't even remember. Still, doesn't she notice he is like a good five or seven years younger than me?*

Alarm dude smiled, obviously flattered over the idea.

Surprising. She thought the old lady knew her business with the amount of time she spent in her rocking chair on the front step watching every move Charly made. "We'll have to talk later." Taking the call and chattering about sex nonstop with a woman of God in the house was not her idea of "a good time to be had by all."

"Okay, I'll call you back," Liz groaned, thankfully not pushing the point.

"I think that's for the best, thank you." She hung up the phone and looked at Mrs. Newman, who was staring at her.

"A friend trying to set you up on a blind date, dear?"

"Sort of." No, Liz and Jenna, her other dear friend, didn't bother. They'd found her a killer townhouse on Hotly Avenue. Other than Mrs. Newman, Charly was the only woman on the street. Why would her friends set her up on a blind date when they had her set up house around hot men? Then her friends would come over and talk about hotter sex while ogling her neighbors. Life was hard for her friends who were both still single.

"You know, I met my husband, God rest his soul, on a blind date." The elderly lady sighed. "I think it's the way heaven gets two people together who wouldn't meet under normal circumstances. God works in mysterious ways."

Charly hoped that was be the message from God Mrs. Newman wanted to share. She somehow doubted it when noticing the battle ready sized scriptures in the woman's hand.

*Why didn't I notice those before? Oh right, thoughts of the knife, and the phone ringing with one of my over-sexed friends.*

Nervously, she glanced at the scriptures

again and knew how the alarm dude felt when he'd seen the knife. She was more scared than he had been. Dear church lady Newman could have used that massive Bible as a body shield. If Charly had to guess, the woman did, to thwart Satan.

*Boy, would she love my artwork. Okay, no, since at every opportunity I get, I portray sin. Liz was right — if you're painting it, you're not doing it.*

She looked to Mrs. Newman's other hand and eyed the plate. She silently swore those brownies were taking in her body and figuring out their strategic attack on which parts they were going to burrow into like cellulite bunnies.

The elderly church lady shook her head and stepped deeper into the living room. "It was so strange the night I went out with him. I had dreaded going out with a total stranger. Only the moment..." A small smile came to her face with a distant look. "I saw that he would be the one I spent my life with."

Charly's heart tightened. The woman had obviously loved her husband, her memories good. That was something Charly would never experience. She had a career. She was rich and famous, sort of. She had a beautiful daughter that she didn't have to share with an ex-husband. Her ex-husband had died three months after they'd divorced when Leigh was two. It was tragic, really, due to eating something that contained shellfish. The son of a bitch had no clue until his severe allergies had closed his throat shut. Charly had it all, but a man? She wasn't looking for one.

Mrs. Newman snapped out of her trance and looked at her as if she had heard her thoughts. "It will happen to you; you will see."

The woman might as well have uttered the words proclaiming death. Charly's heart stopped beating. "I can't see it happening. Actually, I'm not even dating. No prospects in sight."

"I'd like to take you out," the alarm dude piped up. What kind of drugs was he on? He looked maybe five years past legal and he was, well, misfortunate-looking.

She smiled and shook her head, banishing painful images of spending time with the young man in a social setting. "Thanks, but I'm not ready."

He was about to speak in protest.

"Really, I'm not looking." She had to stress her point. He was young and would recover.

"Well... Your name, dear?" Mrs. Newman asked.

"Charly," she answered, thankful for the subject change.

"Well, Charly," Mrs. Newman started. "It always rains when we least expect it." Dark clouds moved in outside the patio doors off the living room, blocking the sunlight with a loud rumble of thunder, a crack of lightning, and a light sprinkle of rain. Then it cleared as quickly as the sudden change in weather had started.

The alarm dude looked puzzled and glanced to the windows. "Weird!"

Acting like she hadn't noticed the bizarre weather, Mrs. Newman set the brownies down next to the computer. Oh, that was good; the aspiring cellulite bunnies in their chocolate camouflage were now located inches away from the keyboard where all Charly's paperwork sat from the gallery. They had their mission and she had hers. They had to be taken out. To the kitchen, of course. She hoped out of sight, out of mind would apply until Leigh could get home and eat the majority of them. Hell, if she poured milk on them in a bowl they could constitute cereal. Not a healthy supper or one of champions, but most definitely it would keep the fat off Charly's ass.

She turned back to the sweet, well-meaning older woman and smiled. What had they been talking about? "I—"

"Well, I must be off now, dear. The Lord has used me as his instrument, and I have left you his song."

*Next time, please bring those little white airplane bags.*

"Oh, that's really too bad." Charly sounded convincing and inched toward the front door in hopes to speed her neighbor's departure along. She sent a silent message to the brownies that they would not overcome and she would prevail over their plan to make her fat.

"I'll be back another time, dear. You and I can have a nice visit then," the dear old lady assured as Charly opened the front door.

"That would be lovely." She thought that would be just too soon. If she could get away with locking the doors and shutting the blinds during that time, she would. Maybe she wouldn't be home, but at the gallery.

"Maybe I'll make you a nice Bundt cake."

Entertained at the notion that people still made Bundt cakes, Charly smiled. Next thing she knew, Mrs. Newman would be there for tea in the afternoons, and nothing would get done at the gallery that was supposed to open three weeks from now.

"A Bundt cake would be perfect for tea." *Now please leave.*

Mrs. Newman looked happy, too happy.

Charly was being set up for some horrific death. Okay, dramatics were getting away. She couldn't picture those battle scriptures coming over without being opened.

"Until then, Charly." Mrs. Newman walked out the door.

*Thank heavens.*

It was all Charly could do not to shut the door, then lock it with a thousand locks similar to that of a character in a cartoon trying to keep another character out. She turned from the now closed door and noticed the alarm dude eyeing her over again. The cartoon scene seemed ever more fitting. Ten locks to keep the church lady out only to realize she had locked herself in with a tiger.

True, the nerdy alarm dude was no tiger, but still. "How are things going?" she asked. She hoped he would be on his way too.

"I'm just attaching the wiring all together so everything is connected electrically." He flashed a smile of metal.

*Charming.*

"I see." It didn't matter how it was connected as long as the alarm kept crazy fans out and her and Leigh safe. Charly didn't care much past that.

"Now, when the alarm goes off, you'll end up with all emergency response here." He put more tools and wires back in his kit.

"Great, I think the whole idea, though, is for the alarm *not* to go off." She really wanted the little alarm weasel to leave. "I'm hoping it will end up being another incident where I overreacted."

"Like greeting people at the door with a knife?" He was trying to be cute, or he was being sarcastic. Either way, his comment was annoying as hell.

She blanched, then growled, "Something like that."

"Well, let me finish up. Then I'll show you everything and give you your code."

"Good idea." Charly smiled and tried to remain calm. "Why don't you do that?"

In less than thirty minutes, the alarm dude was done and out the door. Charly needed a coffee, and walked into the kitchen. She stared at the mug with a cow on it and the ice cold coffee inside. She groaned, knowing it was pointless to pour another cup. She glanced in the heart-shaped dish on the counter that also had a cow on it. It had been originally bought to hold candies. Instead, it ended up as the dump zone for loose change and stray bills shoved into pockets.

Charly needed to burn off the calories her breakfast cookie had carried with it. Not to mention, she had a few dollars change and the motivation it would require for a walk. She scooped a couple dollars out of the tray, debated a minute, and decided to sneak over to the doughnut shop just down the street for a good cup of coffee. She would at least have the slow walk back to enjoy the steaming coffee while it was hot. As a bonus, she decided to try some exotic new flavor.

She quickly ran upstairs, slipped off her

cut-offs, and pulled on the sweatpants that matched the hoodie she had on. In moments, runners were on, the door was locked, and amazingly, she had remembered how to set the alarm. Charly had a good memory. It was just a little short sometimes.

The walk was slightly cool, but the sun shining bright combined with the fresh air seemed to energize her. Maybe she should leave the confinement of her house more often and venture forth. She thought about that a moment and realized that she couldn't see that happening anytime soon. Too much paperwork for the gallery that needed to get done. Not to mention, the gallery itself. When she did venture out, her destinations were either the PTA meeting at the school or the grocery store.

*Life in the fast lane.*

Truthfully, she felt safe inside; outside the walls of the home or gallery felt like the world was watching her. Ironic, since most of the time she didn't think they noticed her. In her opinion, she was far from a woman who turned heads and had men ogle her. She was sure it was because her body was usually covered, and she had an eight-year-old in tow who had a habit to talk nonstop.

Approaching the doughnut shop, she noticed the police car out front. With her luck, officer Cole Scepetti would be here. It would explain why he hadn't made it by yet. He would've found guarding the jelly-filled doughnuts and the honey-glazed doughnut holes a priority. What did she expect out of a cop? They were proving to be as useless here as they had been back in New York.

She sighed and glanced at her reflection in the glass window. She looked like a slob. Dark auburn hair was piled up on her head and fastened in a clip, allowing the curly ends to sprawl out. She had no makeup on, and despite the cookie breakfast, her sweatpants looked big on her. Charly swore she was the only one she knew that could lose weight by eating.

She thought of the plate of brownies. Okay, maybe that was pushing things. There was nothing thinning about the disguised cellulite bunnies, despite what her two dear friends thought about chocolate being the all-round cure all. She would save them for when she had the girls over. Providing Leigh didn't eat them all first.

She pulled open the door of the doughnut shop, thinking about the three of them sitting around drinking wine and eating fattening things. Being back in California with her friends had advantages and disadvantages. Maybe daily walks were not such a bad idea after all. She grunted. Neither were the thoughts of liposuction and a tummy tuck, but those weren't in the immediate future either. Possibly, once she opened the gallery and had a staff she could trust.

Two officers sat by the far window. She was relieved to see that they were both women, and it left her wondering where in the world Skippy the wonder cop was. She knew where he wasn't, and that was seeing that the target of an overzealous fan was safe. The idiot. She was lying in wait for the man of the law. Part of her hoped he wouldn't bother showing up at this point. The other part of her hoped he would. That way, she could be nasty and express her displeasure over his lack of service.

She walked up to the counter and decided on the flavored English Toffee cappuccino. It was exactly what she needed to clear her head. It might even help her find the mental capacity to paint something brilliant, or photograph anything other than Leigh and her friends... Not likely with the MIA muse.

"Can I help you?" an extremely peppy, young blonde behind the counter greeted.

*What is it with happy people?*

"Yes, a large English Toffee, please." Charly forced a smile.

"Would you like a doughnut to go with that? They were all made fresh this morning." She waited patiently behind her little digital cash register.

*Does my ass look like it needs a doughnut*

18

*added to it? No, it's fat enough.*

Had the blonde not noticed that little detail? She bit her tongue, found some manners, and broadened the fake smile. "No, thank you. Just the coffee."

"Are you sure?" the blonde asked again, as if Charly was speaking another language.

"Yes. I'm sure I don't need the calories, or someone pressuring me into a sale of eighty-nine cents. I'm sorry, you'll have to meet your doughnut quota with someone else."

Stunned, the blonde stuck her lips together in a purse, causing her to resemble a fish in more unflattering ways than one would want.

Charly's smile became more genuine. Was it because she had just been a perfect bitch? Possibly—her opportunities these days were so few. Maybe she had a buildup of mean streak. She had no one to be mean to. Except for unsuspecting doughnut chicks that needed to be informed what looks not to give, especially ones that emphasized less appealing features. Doughnut Chick's thin lips would be one of them. Despite the fact that Charly's own lips were currently without lipstick, she was glad that they were still evident by their full pout and cupid's bow.

She quickly passed the young woman with the fish face the money for her purchase and turned away, hoping that there were enough people to witness should the cashier get the urge to spit in the coffee. Charly glanced around, surprised it was so busy for the early afternoon. Did nobody attend work anymore? She sighed and settled her gaze on three very large, very good-looking men.

Hunkies would be the word her friends Jenna and Liz would have used. Two of the three men shifted their attention on her and smiled.

*Had I known someone was going to notice me, I would've run a brush through my hair and taken the two minutes out for makeup. Too late, the damage is done.*

Charly went to turn away when the third man with them looked up and stared right at her. Never in a million years was this supposed to happen, not now. She blinked at the familiar face and her heart sank to the floor. How in the world had this happened? More importantly, what was he doing there?

## Chapter Two

Charly gazed into the most brilliant green eyes. They held a sparkle to them that she didn't quite remember as the man they belonged to walked to where she stood transfixed. She turned to see an older woman and her husband walk from the peppy cashier with the fish lips. "Pinch me, I think I'm dreaming," Charly muttered under her breath as her high school crush approached.

"I'll pinch her," the older man whispered.

"You touch her ass and I'll make your life hell," the older woman told her husband.

"What else would be new?" he grumbled back.

The laughter and snickers coming from the three men caught Charly off guard and drew her attention back to them. She stared back into those intense green eyes. "This is such a surprise," the owner of the voice told her.

"Isn't it though?" she managed to mutter out. She sounded like she was rambling, yet she could barely speak. Intelligent thoughts were required. She couldn't be that nervous schoolgirl. "Jason Prescott, how have you been?" That was a hell of a start.

"I'm great, even better after seeing you, a familiar face. How have you been, Charlene?"

He reminded her in some strange way this wasn't a dream. Then again, considering how she looked, a better word would be nightmare.

"Fine, wow! Jason, I go by Charly now. What are you doing here?" She was still stunned, and trying not to act horrified over the fact that she looked like she belonged behind a metal tub with a washboard.

"I just got traded to the Anaheim Angels and now I'm living here in Irvine during the off season." He looked puzzled, but he was sexy; he was allowed to look anyway he wanted. Why didn't she remember him being this good-looking? "What are you doing here? Liz told me that you moved to New York. That was about seven years ago now."

"I live here," she stammered. She didn't want to notice that he was no longer the high school guy, but a very built man. "I mean, I moved back with my daughter not that long ago."

His smile broadened and revealed his deep dimples. "What are the chances?"

Charly didn't want to panic. Was that a skill-testing question? "Who would believe?"

"Maybe it's fate."

*Fate is a bitch then for letting me leave the house looking like this.*

"Listen, I have to get to practice, but I'd love your number and to go out sometime." He looked surprised and unsure. Where were

22

these expressions coming from? She had never known Jason to look unsure once during their four years of high school. "I mean, if your husband wouldn't mind?"

"No, he won't." *What the hell?* "I mean, I don't have a husband, or anyone else to complicate my life."

"If I won't complicate things too much, I would love to go out."

*That was sweet; points for the baseball player.*

Charly smiled sincerely. "I'd like that."

He nodded and pulled out a piece of paper from his pocket. He then helped himself to a pen on the order counter and stopped the bimbo blonde-haired woman from commenting by flashing a killer smile. He turned back to Charly. "Now, what's your number?"

She rattled off her number. "I was just thinking about you the other day."

"Well, sweetie, you've crossed my mind more than once over the years. I'm glad to see you. Anyhow, baseball practice beckons."

"Pro-ball, wow! Good, that's a long way from high school." She shouldn't have said that. Damn her lack of verbal thought process.

His eyes started at Charly's hair caught in the clip and took their time taking in every detail of her as they moved over her body.

*Oh dear!*

His green eyes met her brown ones again and he smiled. "You've come a long way too."

He shoved the paper he had written her number on into his pocket. The chances were high the jeans would hit a wash cycle and he would never call. He cast a wink, causing her heart to slam into her throat. "I'll call you soon."

"I hope so," she whispered. *Where the hell is my voice? Oh! Right, gone with all reason.*

"You can count on it." He walked away with his hunky friends.

Charly couldn't help but feel a little stunned. The girls would never believe this one. She could almost hear her friends now. Liz, the outgoing and sensual one, was the loudest, filling her ears with comments. Liz would remember Jason from high school. He had been on her list of guys to kiss. Then there was Jenna. Yes, she would no doubt have comments too.

"Your English Toffee," the blonde behind the counter voiced, and cut into her thoughts like a knife through a cake. A yummy, extra calories, triple layer chocolate cake.

"Thank you." She lifted the coffee and didn't care if the blonde had spit in it or not. She was still surprised over running into the dreamy third baseman from high school, now all grown up and even yummier.

Charly crossed the doughnut shop floor to the entrance and her spirits brightened a notch. Things were looking up. Now, to see if

Jason would really call. If anything, things would be interesting — of course, that was an understatement. She did know that Jason had seemed genuinely attracted. That was a concept Charly was having a hard time wrapping her brain around. The man hadn't noticed her in high school when she was drop-dead gorgeous. Now that she had the frumpy housewife look down, the man seemed interested. The whole incident drove home her theory even further. Men made zero sense.

Home before she knew it, Charly barely remembered the walk. She'd been so wrapped up in her thoughts that it wasn't until she crossed over the threshold in a mad dash to the ringing house phone that she noticed she had almost finished her coffee.

After wasting her day in productive and distracting ways, like talking to Jenna then Liz on the phone, Charly had been able to fit in a couple calls from out-of-state clients wanting new pieces of work. Leigh got home from school, and then the battle over her spelling words began. Dinner was in the oven.

Charly was still smiling over her run-in with Jason and the fact that the man may or may not call. He was hunky eye candy and the fact he wanted her number alone could keep her happy for days.

It was, overall, a good day, despite the fact

she hadn't gotten anything painted. It was official, her muse was never coming home. She would never be able to fill clients' orders with a brilliant paint stroke, or anything, which left her with a niggling sensation of doom. Charly was going to end up having to take a chance on more artists' works to fill her shop. The horror poured over her; she was going to be just a store owner and not the sexy, mysterious, never-shown-her-face-to-the-world Joey Sinn.

Joey Sinn was the woman every man wanted. Women couldn't help but love her and want to be like her. She captured the naked form, lust, and desire in paintings like no other. That wasn't the case anymore. No romance and no passion. If Charly didn't find inspiration soon, she was in danger of Joey Sinn—the clever alias of an abbreviated middle name—falling from the artistic world. Things were worse than she imagined. There was no way she could let that happen. She needed inspiration, and fast.

Maybe it was Charly's artistic side, or maybe she had been a single mom for too long. There were days, though, it seemed that an angel sat on one of her shoulders and a devil sat on the other. Currently, the devil on her one shoulder laughed, making a rude comment about her needing to have sex. The angel on the other side huffed, telling her she should give prayer a try. Prayer? At a time like this? Okay, Charly had thrown pleas up to the heavens, but official down-on-her-knees prayer? Not likely that was going to happen anytime soon.

*"I wouldn't be so sure about that,"* a voice whispered into her ears and heart. She got the distinct feeling she had just tempted fate. Then again, what in life was worth tempting if not fate itself?

The phone ringing cut into her thoughts of debate. The thing never stopped ringing. Had she just jinxed herself by inviting fate to throw a curve ball into her life, or was she being her usual paranoid self?

She raced to the phone. "Hello?" She was holding her breath. Was it Jason?

"You have a sexy voice; what are you wearing?" her friend Jenna teased from the other end of the receiver. Trust her to be a comedian.

"Ha, ha, what a laugh and a half you are. What did you do, quit your job and take to the road with a comedy routine?" Charly glanced at the oven and wondered if the yummy-smelling chicken was ready. She couldn't remember eating anything other than the cookie that morning and drinking countless cups of coffee.

"My, don't we sound pleasant. What's up with you?" Jenna asked. The woman had only called two other times that day.

"I think my spirituality is lacking," Charly confessed, and headed toward the oven.

"You're worried about your spirituality, that's new. Tell me, do you go out of your way to find new and exciting things to worry about?" This coming from a woman who hardly ever worried. Oh, to be like that. Then again, for a woman who dodged commitment to any writing project past a thousand word column, and any man after a week, Charly knew the answer. Jenna was a great friend. Jenna was a brilliant writer, especially about sex in her monthly column for a prestigious magazine. Jenna was horrible about moving past a one-night-stand and onto a relationship.

Charly scowled at her remark, though it almost seemed a waste since Jenna wasn't there to see it. "I don't sit and think things up to worry about."

"Right, and I haven't had sex in a year." She snorted and giggled.

"What about that young guy that you couldn't get rid of? That was what, five weeks ago?" She opened the oven door to retrieve the baking sheet of chicken and the corning ware dish that had the flavored wild rice.

"That would be my point, Charly."

"Again, a comedian. Jenna, you're on a roll."

A loud beeping started. "Mom's cooking!"

Leigh called as she hurried down the stairs and over to the fire alarm that was rapidly going off. It always did when she cooked. Not that Charly burned food. It just seemed to like going off when the oven door opened.

"Nice, you're burning down your house. Good one, Charly," Jenna commented as Leigh opened the front door.

*The smoke detector has issues.*

"Actually, it does that every time the door is opened when the oven's on. I swear the thing hates me. It must be male."

"Sure, I bet. In truth, you got distracted and burned dinner." Jenna laughed as a ringing started.

"No!" The ringing grew louder, and her mind raced trying to make logic of the sound.

"Oh hell!" Charly breathed in horror. "The alarm system is wired into the smoke detector."

Jenna snorted. "And I would care why? Thanks for sharing."

"Because the smoke detector is wired to the alarm in case there is a break in—which means all emergency response is going to be showing up at my house." She knew what the ringing was. It was a siren, and she knew where it was headed. Straight to her address.

Jenna inhaled deep from the other end of the phone, thankfully quiet for a moment as Charly collected her thoughts. "Wait!" And the quiet lasted maybe a whole minute. "You mean to tell me you're going to have men in uniform arrive at your house?"

Charly groaned. "Yes, that's exactly what I'm saying."

"Why are you so lucky? All you're going to do is paint pictures of them."

Seriously? That was Jenna's main concern? "I don't think I'll be doing that. Explaining myself is holding possibilities."

"Cool!" Leigh squealed. "There's a police car and a fire truck. Mom, there are firemen!" Leigh was delighted. "And hotty officers."

"Leigh, show some respect." She had Jenna and Liz to thank for that word becoming part of Leigh's vocabulary.

"What's happening?" Jenna demanded from the other end of the phone.

"Nothing, just emergency response. Fireman and officers and medics, oh my."

"You have hot men there? In uniform?" Jenna demanded, suddenly more than interested.

"No, Jenna, they showed up naked." She silently wondered where her friend's head was. On second thought, she had some ideas and bit her tongue to prevent asking for confirmation.

"Now who's being the comedian?" her friend snorted with feigned hurt.

"Come on, honey. Let's get you out of the

house," Charly heard a deep, sexy voice say as a large frame blocked her view of her daughter.

"No, it's okay," Leigh told the fully dressed fireman as two more came up behind with a hose to the entrance. "My mom was just cooking. This is cool. You guys have never come before and Mom sets the alarm off almost nightly. Except when we have sandwiches and doughnuts for dinner."

"Your mom was cooking?" the fireman asked as he turned toward Charly. He removed his oxygen mask.

Her breath caught. He was the best looking man she had ever seen. She closed her parted lips.

"What's happening? I hear male voices. So help me, Charly, don't abandon me. I want every glorious detail. Are they yummy?"

"Oh yes, there are hardly words." She took in amazingly blue eyes as the large, well-built fireman took off his helmet. "Wow!" Her voice was barely a whisper.

"Wow? They're hot, aren't they? So help me, say something, Charly." Jenna was having a curiosity is killing the cat breakdown on the other end of the phone.

"Well, I can see everything is in order," the incredibly sexy fireman told her with a grin. His dark hair intensified his eyes. His smile could cause more than one sprinkler system to go off from the raw, male heat. Charly wished *she* had a sprinkler system because her body temperature had just shot up—about twenty degrees.

His eyes dragged over her with an expression that noted every detail. She might be out of the loop where men were concerned, but a look that blatant and that interested was a little hard to miss.

"You're breathing funny!" Jenna screamed in her ear. "Tell me!"

"Hi," Charly greeted, amazed that she could speak.

"Hi. I see that we had a minor incident with the oven." He stepped closer. Her grip tightened on the phone. Her palms were starting to sweat.

"Is that man as sexy as he sounds? My panties are wet from just the sound of him. Charly, answer me. This this is the most action I've had in a while."

"Yes," she answered both the hot fireman and her friend.

"Damn it! I knew I should've come over. I would be there. I would have caused a lot more than that alarm to go off. I'd be busy working on that no doubt delicious flame fighter of a man."

Charly caught Jenna's words, but the fireman was truly hot and currently holding her attention.

"Everything looks fine," he told her in what she was guessed was his expert opinion. However, the way he smiled at her, and ran his gaze over her body again, gave Charly the distinct impression he was referring to more than the lack of flames and the shake-and-bake chicken now sitting on the stove.

"I know that tone. He's checking you out, isn't he?" The woman had zero patience at times.

"Oh yes." She tried to keep her answer to Jenna non-revealing.

"Wow, this chicken looks and smells great." The firefighter walked over to the crispy, coated poultry, followed by two of his fellow flame fighters.

"That is man language for him telling you he thinks you're hot," Jenna yelled as if Charly needed a translator. The man had spoken English, and as far as Charly could recall, she had understood every word he had just spoken.

"I don't think so." She tried to regain her ability to breathe.

"No, really, this looks good." The firefighter must have thought that she had been talking to him.

Leigh came flying into the kitchen. "You should all have some, and Mom always has leftovers.

The sexy man smiled at Leigh. "We

possibly couldn't."

"Sure you can. The chicken is dead and baked, so it can't bite. Help yourself. I will get plates for the rice."

All Charly could do was stare at the scene unfolding in her kitchen.

"Dive in," Leigh told the men. "Better to eat while it's hot, or so Mom says."

The sexy man and his friends chuckled, then he took off a thick, large glove and reached for a chicken thigh.

Jenna groaned. "I need details, Charly!"

The firefighter's sexy lips touched the chicken and he bit into it while the other two firefighters followed suit.

*Oh, this is not happening.*

"This chicken is really great!" He smiled. Her heart slammed to a dead stop. If she dropped from heart failure, he could always resuscitate her, right?

"He's eating the chicken? Damn it, Charly." Oh yeah, Jenna was having a fit alright. "Throw your ass on a plate and serve yourself up next to it." There was a pause. "Hell, just tell him to help himself."

"Thank you," she muttered to the sexy fireman. It worked as a response to Jenna as well.

There were footsteps crossing the threshold; someone else had just walked in. "Hi!" Leigh greeted. "Should I get you a plate too?"

Charly glanced to where the new arrival stood on the inside of the front entrance threshold, and she noticed the uniform. "And in walk the police."

"Oh man, you're having a buffet and I'm thirty miles away thinking what a bitch you are." Jenna laughed. "Let me guess, he's hot too."

"You guys should try this chicken," the fireman called out to the two who were standing there watching the floorshow.

"Oh God, no," Charly groaned as she read the last name on the officer's uniform.

"What? He's not hot?" There was a sound in the background at her end. Jenna was popping popcorn?

"Oh yes, he is." The officer turned around. Oh, he was sexy all right. "Unbelievable!" she whispered, both over the fact her friend found this entertaining enough to make snack food, and over the fact she was now staring at the drop-dead gorgeous Officer Cole Scepetti. "Jenna, I'll call you back!" Her eyes never left the officer about to meet her wrath.

"Why? What's wrong? Is the officer hotter than the fireman? If he is, you can give him dessert."

"It's Skippy," she stammered.

"What does peanut..." There was a pause. Charly counted the seconds. "You mean

Skippy, the lazy cop?"

*Wow, three seconds. A new record for Jenna.*
She turned into the living room to put the
phone back on the base.

"Give him hell, Charly, but don't get
arrested. Do you want me to call Liz and let
her know that you'll be calling for bail?"

"Goodbye," she answered in response,
and hung up the phone.

She glanced from the coffee table in the
living room to the kitchen to see the firemen
gathered around the chicken, eating by the
stove. Leigh had joined them and had sure
enough not only given them plates, but had
gotten them forks. Charly was quite sure this
wasn't in their policy and procedures.

"I see that it's a false alarm."

She turned to the officer as he walked his
tall, well-built frame into the living room.

Normally, there was no way she'd meet
an officer of the law looking like she did
currently. Tonight was different, however. She
had been checked out by two hotties. The
fireman was of similar build to the delicious
officer, but his eyes...

She shook images of the gorgeous,
chicken-eating fireman out of her mind. Her
temper toward the officer in question had
peaked. And currently, she didn't care how
good-looking he was. "Well, if it isn't the
infamous Officer Scepetti."

"Have we met?" He looked puzzled. It drove home the fact that he was cute and confused.

Charly sighed and crossed her arms across her chest. "No, not officially. We probably would have *if* you were up to speed on things, and *if* you had come by to do my safety check."

His dark gaze fell on her. He was thinking. She silently wondered if it was a hard task for him. "What's your name?"

Charly lifted her brows and glared. "Charlene. I'm from New York. They called out here to arrange for my safety and assured me that you would come by and check on me. To make sure that my house was safe for my daughter and me."

"I don't recall." He looked sincere.

"Apparently, you don't check your email or return calls either," she informed, a little bit snottier than she should have.

"I've been busy. It must have slipped my mind." He didn't look amused over her attitude. It sucked to be him.

"It's a good thing that deranged stalker of a fan has not 'slipped' into my house and killed or hurt my daughter and me." She was mad. Who did he think he was?

"You don't need to be hostile." He moved his hands as if to shove the air down, as well as her temper.

"You have no idea what hostile is for me." She knew damn well it was pushing her luck.

"Is that a threat?" He narrowed his gaze on her.

"Don't flatter yourself," Charly replied before thinking.

*Okay, not wise to say.*

She was hoping that Jenna had called Liz. That way when she called Liz from a holding cell, she wouldn't be surprised.

"Don't be rude," he scolded in an offended tone.

"Forgive me if I'm not happy with you. I was scared and counted on you. You never bothered to do your job. I left countless messages for you, had them email you, and still no word. I was ready to send you a highlighted map with directions to my house so you wouldn't get lost."

Officer Gorgeous glanced around. "I guess you got the alarm system. Is it part of our program?"

Was this guy for real? "No! You see, in order to qualify for such things, I would have had to know the stalker's name and at least give a description."

He furrowed his brows. "Stalkers are serious business."

Without thinking, her palm made contact with her forehead. Oh yeah, she was heading to jail, most likely for assaulting an officer

38

because the next thing her hand came in contact with would be the face of the lawman. "Gee, thank you for clarifying."

"I would be happy to get a statement now, if you want. That way, if there is a problem, we can move forward from there."

She stared at him in disbelief. "So, in addition to your lack of response, hearing is an issue too? Were you not listening to me?" The man was pissing her off in the worst way. "I'm not going to say a damn thing to you. You were the one that your department assigned to keep me safe. So if you want a statement, try 'get your ass out of my house.'"

"Is there a problem in here?" The sexy fireman moved into the room and stood next to her. The temperature of the room shot up.

She scowled at the officer and looked to the fireman. "No, no problem. A certain officer was just leaving."

"Hi, Cole." The sexy firefighter greeted the thorn-in-her-side man of the law. Thorn was the wrong word. Nasty pain-in-the-ass was a better phrase.

"Hi, Ethan. How was the chicken?" Both men apparently forgot she was in the room.

"It was great. She certainly can cook." He turned and smiled at her. He was a hunk and a half. Her heart was beating again, but it was at an unhealthy speed.

"Thank you," she answered. Her cheeks

warmed as they undoubtedly tinted with pink. "I'm Charly." She stuck out her hand, which he shook right away. "I'm sorry about the false alarm." Heat traveled up her arm, and desire flickered over her skin like a hungered tongue.

"I'm sorry we ate the chicken. Your daughter is cute."

"No worries about the chicken. I'm glad you enjoyed it. My daughter has her moments."

He smiled. "I'm Ethan."

"Well, since everything is fine, we should get the hose out of the hall and allow this fine woman to feed her child," Cole informed them as Ethan and Charly stood and stared at each other.

"She already ate. She ate with us," Ethan answered, but kept his eyes on her. "Don't worry about the alarm."

"False alarms are a serious offense," the annoying officer reminded.

Charly turned and glared at the officer. "Thank you for the reminder of the law. For a man that is so busy, don't you have something to do other than be here?"

He scowled. "I'm glad you have your alarm. Good luck. Call me if you need anything."

*Like that will do me any good!* She didn't bother responding. Instead, she watched him leave and turned to Ethan.

He studied her and glanced to the kitchen before returning his attention on her. "We better go too. Don't hesitate to call nine-one-one if there's a problem."

She nodded as he walked back into the kitchen. As if on cue, her phone rang. She reached and picked it up as Leigh saw the men out with lots of goodbyes. Charly couldn't see her, but knew she was waving. Happy, congenial child. So unlike her mother. "Hello?"

"Okay, are they gone?" Jenna asked in curiosity.

"Yes." Charly sighed, she couldn't believe her day.

"Good, because I want every last, juicy detail," she informed. There was a light crunching sound. She was eating the popcorn.

Charly threw herself onto the sofa and tried to digest everything that had just taken place. "You're never going to believe this — but on the bright side, I'm not on my way to a police station."

## Chapter Three

Charly woke to the loud and irritating sound of yard equipment. "Whoever the insensitive soul with the lawnmower and leaf blower is, he is going to die a slow and painful death." She glanced to the alarm clock. It was six-fifteen on a Friday morning and she was talking to herself. "Make that painful and cruel death."

It was official, she was losing her mind. She reached to the side of her bed that was undisturbed and grabbed the hair clip that she had tossed next to the alarm clock. She decided to head down the stairs and make coffee. A smart woman would realize she needed to get more sleep, but she couldn't see that happening anytime soon. Before sleep could happen, she had to feel calm and safe.

Her heart tightened at the mess the house was in as she moved to the hall and slowly descended the stairs. She supposed she should clean up a bit. It wasn't like the place was dirty, just horribly untidy; the situation might be improved if she finished unpacking boxes. With a sigh, she picked up the school bag that her charming daughter had dropped on the floor and the coat draped over the banister. Oh yes, life had to get better than this. She would need a housekeeper once the gallery opened.

Charly walked into the kitchen and went to flip on the light. It didn't come on. Not even a flicker of illumination. She remembered she still hadn't fixed the fixture since she highly doubted it was the bulb. Once she remembered to make a to-do list, she would have to add fixing the light to that ever growing list—provided she remembered. With her luck, she would forget it until she needed it—like now.

"Maybe I'll just call someone," she told the Winnie the Pooh cookie jar. There was a lot she had to do, but seemed low on energy and time. She went through the motions and made the coffee. She hardly slept. Often, she just laid in bed awake trying to think of something fresh and exciting to paint.

"I need something brilliant before I start getting more orders for the scandalous artwork of Joey Sinn." The yellow bear looked like it was laughing at her. She was crazy. She was holding conversations with cookie jars that couldn't talk. Certainly not a sign of good mental health.

She closed her eyes and thought long and hard for an erotic image to dance through her mind. Nothing came other than the grocery list and the things she still had to do at the gallery, which was just empty retail space. She was more than a little screwed and it had nothing to do with hot male bodies.

Right away, an image of sparkling blue eyes came to her mind. *Ethan.* She could only imagine that man's body under his heavy, fire retardant coat. Her body tingled at recollection how handsome he was. No man had a right to be that gorgeous and have eyes that striking. He was, in theory, supposed to put out fires, not start them on looks alone.

She opened her eyes and stared at the dark liquid emptying down into the glass pot. She had lost all lucid thought, as she was seriously debating asking one of her hot and sexy neighbors to get naked and inspire. Maybe Jenna and Liz were right; maybe she needed to have real sex. Her brows lifted, but she couldn't imagine having sex with one of her male naked models in a hungry animal sex sort of way... She scowled and Ethan's face flashed to mind again. Why was it that an image of the ever-hunky fireman raced to mind when she thought of sex?

With a snort, Charly headed off to the computer to check her email for Joey Sinn. In a perfect world, there would be no emails. She grunted and pictured at least a dozen that would need immediate attention. What were the chances? *Slim to none,* the annoying little devil on her shoulder piped up. *Don't be paranoid,* the angel rebuffed in response. She silently willed them both to shut up and opened the email account. Five new emails. A whimper filled the room and she knew the pathetic sound had left her lips. Two of the correspondences were from very good customers who would undoubtedly want another fabulous original painting.

"Joey Sinn is dead, people. I killed her." She smiled at her own humor, which in reality, wasn't even funny.

The doorbell went and she sighed. *Now what? And who this early in the morning?*

She got up from the computer, then walked toward the front door and paused, glancing into the kitchen at the knife block. Charly opted to go over to the door weapon free. She had just become brave, was real tired, had a gallery to put together, not to mention was still trying to think of something dazzling to paint. Should it be someone wanting to hurt her, the bad person might be doing her a favor at this point.

She glanced at the lock on the door and noticed it was latched, even more reason to be brave. Charly peeked through the blinds to see that the possible bad guy was actually the delicious officer Cole. She groaned and rolled her eyes. Reaching for the lock, she remembered she was in pajamas. There were days she had no luck. Come to think of it, she had weeks and even months like that. Maybe it was a sign that the man should see her dressed for bed. What the hell was she thinking? She didn't believe in signs. Mrs. Newman was going to have to stop coming over.

She shook the thought of bedding the unworthy officer out of her mind as she undid the lock and opened the door. Charly was still not happy with the man for not being around when she had first moved in and had been scared. "Good morning, officer. What a surprise. The doughnut shop is three blocks over. If you want, you can walk it."

Not even six-thirty in the morning and her crusade to get arrested prevailed. Hopefully, she would get arrested for ego bashing *after* Leigh went to school.

Officer Cole Scepetti wasn't amused, but smiled. "Charlene, it's good to see you in such a good mood."

She smiled insincerely. "Don't call me Charlene. It's Charly or nothing at all. What can I say?" Oh yeah, she was out to push his buttons. Who knew, it might even become a new hobby for her. "You, officer, bring out the finer qualities of my personality."

"I'd hate to see the less than sweet ones." Even while he grimaced, he looked handsome. Mother Nature was a twisted lady with a warped sense of humor.

"No worries. You just got here and the morning is still young. Lots of opportunity, I'd say." Maybe she should call Jenna or Liz to come over now in case her trip to a holding cell preceded Leigh getting out the door for the school bus.

"Need I remind you, I'm an officer of the law?" he asked, showing his lack of entertainment at her comebacks.

"Actually, I'm glad that you cleared that up."

*Oh yeah, getting arrested for sure.*

She was bitter, and that was putting it mildly. "I think it's your lack of professionalism that confused me as to your actual job description."

"You're not a morning person, are you?" He tilted his head slightly and squared his jaw. Again, he shouldn't have looked that sexy and she shouldn't have noticed.

"Quite the contrary, I think you're confusing it with me being not really a cop friendly person

"That was honest."

"Yes. Forgive me. I've been accused of being somewhat to the point."

He nodded. "I would use the word blunt."

"Feel free to use what you need to make yourself feel better." Charly took in his appearance. His dark brown hair and long black lashes suited the dark brown of his eyes. A strange flutter moved in her stomach and she shook it off. "Now, what is so important that finally, six weeks later, you can find my house and insist on keeping me from a hot cup of coffee?"

"Actually, I was hoping to talk to you." He looked unsure of himself.

It was mean, but she reveled in his self-doubt. She saw it as a perfect opportunity to push his buttons harder. "Talk, you mean conversation more intriguing and stimulating than this?"

"Can you please cut me some slack?" He looked like his patience was thinning.

"I believe that's what I did for six weeks." She might have wanted to rethink that comment through before speaking, but too late now.

"It was me not doing your safety check that I wanted to talk to you about." He glanced down at the cement step and then brought his dark gaze up to her.

She inhaled deep. "I have the alarm system. So, you and your law enforcing butt can be hero somewhere else."

"I wanted to apologize." The cutie officer looked serious and sincere standing in his designer jeans and light powder blue button-down shirt.

"And I wanted a coffee," she replied, knowing she couldn't keep being mean to him. He was cute and he did look sorry. "Maybe you would like to come in for a minute and we can be civil over coffee?" Her cell phone started ringing. Correction, the cell phone she used as Joey Sinn started ringing.

He nodded, allowing her to back away from the door and swoop to the computer to shut the screen down so it was not in view. She opted to let her cell phone ring.

The front door closed. "Are you going to answer that?"

She looked at the officer now standing in the living room at the bottom of the stairs. "No, I want to give you my complete attention if you are going to grace me with an apology."

He smiled weakly as they stood there staring at each other. His gaze shifted over the baggy satin pajamas. He grinned and his expression wasn't that of an arrogant officer, but of a guy interested in a girl.

"You really have a sharp tongue, don't you?" The twinkle in his eyes made him downright sexy and inclined her to believe he was interested in more than just coffee. Oh, right. She had offered him coffee. "What do you take in your coffee?"

He smiled again and she reminded herself he was just a man. Charly's heart picked up speed a notch. "Just sugar."

The tension thickened in the room. "Just sugar it shall be." She walked into the kitchen.

*Was Skippy hitting on me?*

No, she was just really tired. She needed to get lucid thought back.

Charly reached in the cupboard, pulled out a mug, and turned to the coffee pot where her mug was already parked on the counter in front of it.

Footsteps behind her caused her to see the apologetic and yummy-looking Officer Cole lean against the kitchen wall. "I'm sorry about not coming to follow up. I talked to New York. Your stalker is quite persistent from the report. I also know that the identity is unknown."

Charly was sure she had mentioned this all last night. Right. Cute, confused, and deaf. How quickly she forgot.

"Yes." She poured the coffees, added sugar to his, stirred, and passed it to him.

"Thanks."

"You're welcome." She turned back to her mug and proceeded to the fridge where she hauled out the flavored creamer before she returned over to her mug. "So, you wanted to apologize."

"Yeah, I'm sorry. Actually, I think we should sit down over dinner and discuss what we can do to ensure you and your daughter's safety."

Having finished stirring the creamer into her mug, she turned and blinked at him in disbelief as she placed the spoon down and picked up the mug. "Now you want me to cook you dinner?"

He smiled. Okay, yeah, he was cute. "Not exactly, Charly. Though I know the guys at the fire station were still raving about the chicken." He shifted his stance and she couldn't help but notice he had strong legs beneath the designer denim. I want to take you to dinner. My way of saying sorry and giving us a chance to talk without your daughter overhearing."

Charly was shocked. She closed her parted lips and digested this. "You want to take me out to discuss this?"

"I do," he answered, and lifted his mug up to his lips. He had really nice-looking lips. Not that she had noticed; she was mad at him. Great, first talking to herself and now lying to herself. She needed a shrink.

"Fine, I'll go to dinner with you to discuss things away from Leigh." She didn't want to worry her daughter any more than she was. Charly knew Leigh still worried about the stalker finding them.

"Great, it's a date." He reveled in the moment with a Cheshire grin. "How's tomorrow night?"

No, not a date. It was dinner and her safety. She was willing to let the good officer think whatever he wanted. It was Charly that was going to have to explain this to her friends. "Sounds wonderful."

Charly sat at her computer and worked on what she would need in order to get the gallery ready when her cell phone rang. She glanced at it with minor worry and a great deal of contempt. "Sorry, Joey Sinn can't come to the phone right now. Her muse is dead." She reached for the phone and glanced at the all too familiar number. "Joey Sinn," she greeted. *You're so going to hell!* the angel on her one shoulder piped up. The devil on the other shoulder laughed.

"Joey!" Kendra Kensington droned with her ostentatious air. "Thank heavens! I'm having a major crisis, and you, my darling, are the only cure."

Charly rolled her eyes. Kendra Kensington was rich, really rich—the kind of rich where more money than brains applied. She was also overly dramatic. "Kendra, what is the latest fiasco?"

"Well, I was having a small dinner party here the other night. You know, just twenty or thirty people."

*Right, small.*

"And my guests were raving over the last painting you did for me. You know the one. The delicious-looking male with the angel wings sprawled out."

"I remember," Charly replied. Of course she remembered; she had made fifteen thousand off that piece. "So, what's the crisis?

It didn't get damaged, did it?" She loathed touch up work.

"No, not at all, darling. In fact, all the women were in awe over the size of the angel's, well, *divinity* and then Sylvia Mayers told me that you did a larger picture of a downright scrumptious male for her. A knight in shining armor—well, he was more out of it, but he had a big sword." Kendra sounded put out.

Sylvia Mayers was another one with too much money and too much time on her hands. She had also paid Joey twenty-five thousand dollars. It was amazing what women would pay for painted pictures of naked men with a creative twist and a large...sword. Joey Sinn was turning into a legend in the art world. She was a mystery, a curiosity, and most of all, made good money. Charly knew this, being Joey Sinn. She cashed the checks.

"Okay, Kendra, how can I make your day all happy and fix this?"

"I want an almost wall-sized picture. I want it hot, very male, maybe one of your intimate couple ones, and climactic. It has to be climatic ," Kendra was quick to respond. "I want my underwear to soak when I look at that picture. I want sex, Joey. I want it all."

Of course she did. "I'm not sure, Kendra." Doubt and dread chilled her to the bone and her stomach tightened.

*One can't paint without inspiration.*

"Now, Joey, don't be shy. Give me a price," Kendra coaxed with a click of her tongue. "You know what, I'll make this easy. How is, say, two hundred and fifty thousand?"

*Holy hell!* That would pay off what she owed on the townhouse and her new pick-up truck. "Well, I wouldn't be able to have it ready right away. Charly is opening a new gallery here and I'm helping her."

"Joey!" Kendra groaned with pretention. "I'm throwing myself at your mercy. I understand Charly is busy with her gallery. Speaking of which, I'm on the guest list, right? I need a holiday. Could you maybe have it ready for the gallery opening?"

Charly sighed. No, she couldn't have it ready. Hell, she hadn't even lifted a paintbrush to paint walls, let alone a picture. *It's two hundred and fifty thousand dollars!* the devil on her shoulder screamed loudly. *You have an MIA muse. Don't make promises you can't keep,* the angel on the other side scolded.

"The gallery opening is three weeks away. I'll have the painting ready and make sure Charly has you on the guest list." Charly blinked. That sounded slightly schizophrenic, since Joey was Charly and Charly was Joey. What had she been thinking? Oh, right, that she wanted to paint orgasmic pictures of men and couples in a variety of sexual and imaginative scenarios where pleasure prevailed. Without getting kicked off the PTA.

Of course, her super sinful ones always stayed out of the gallery and always went to the homes of clients immediately upon completion. With Leigh in the house, there were some things she didn't need her eight-year-old seeing. So they were kept out of her curious daughter's view.

"Joey, you truly are incredible. I'll be sure to be there with jewelry on and my flirtiest smile ever. I am looking for another husband, you know, so have Charly invite some great candidates. Thank you for helping me out on this."

*And thank you for paying off my house.* "You're welcome."

"Call me next week. Say hi to Charly for me. Take care, darling!" Kendra made a kiss sound and ended the call.

Charly closed the phone and hung her head. The money was good. Other than an MIA muse, she had more serious problems. Where the hell was she going to paint something so large? This was, officially, professional suicide.

The house phone started ringing. She jumped out of her chair and answered it on the second ring. "Hello?"

"Hey, Charlene, err, I guess you go by Charly now," Jason Prescott's sexy voice greeted from the other end of the phone.

Swallowing hard, her heart beat a little faster. "Hi, Jason."

"I hope this isn't a bad time."

"No, not at all." She carried the phone into the kitchen, deciding to pop a couple slices of bread into the toaster, then headed back to the living room.

"Good, I was just wondering if you were free for supper tonight?" He sounded nervous. It was cute.

She already knew Liz or Jenna would babysit if it meant Charly would get out of the house and possibly a social—or a sex life. "Sure, that sounds good."

"Really?" Shock echoed from the other end of the phone. "Wow! Okay, great. I wasn't sure if you'd go out with me."

Another cute and clueless one. What was Mother Nature thinking? "I'd love to."

"Fantastic." Jason sounded thrilled. "How about I pick you up at seven?"

"Seven works," Charly answered.

"Great, go ahead and give me your address."

Charly rattled off the address and sighed. There were other male voices in the background. "This will be fun."

"I'm looking forward to it. I have to get to practice now, but I wanted to call you." He paused. "I wish I had time to talk."

"We can talk over dinner. I suppose I should let you go." *Not that I want to since you have a sexy voice. Not as sexy as Ethan's, but sexy.* Why was she always thinking of the firefighter? It was getting to be an addiction.

"All right, I'll see you tonight at seven." He paused again. "I'm really glad that I ran into you the other day."

Her lips curled into a grin from the sweetness and sincerity of his words. "Me too."

"You know, Charly, I really think there is a reason we caught up after all this time."

*You're hot, and I need sex.*

Images of Jason's hot, naked body played out in her mind. Unfortunately, she just pictured him naked, but didn't picture anything close to resembling sex. "I'll see you tonight." She hung up the phone and smiled a little more. This was going to be a good day.

Inhaling deeply, she wondered what that smell was. It was like something was burning. The high-pitched sound of the fire alarm going off entered her ears. She tore into the kitchen to see smoke filling the kitchen from the small appliance she had shoved the bread into.

She had never used the toaster in the three weeks she had been there. It was a new toaster; it shouldn't burn things. Instinctively, she grabbed a terry tea towel and started fanning the smoke out of the way. The burnt pieces of charcoal shot up and out of the metal slots on the toaster, reminding her that at one time, soft, fresh, multigrain bread had entered.

Charly glanced at the settings on the toaster. Now, had she been paying attention, she would have noticed that they were not set to golden brown. They were, however, set to what she was quite sure was the "cremate" setting. She groaned and glanced at the black corpses of multigrain, now dearly departed. Was it some sign that her body didn't need those yummy, buttered carbs? Quite possibly.

She stomped to the front door and pulled it open to air out the house.

With a sigh, she walked over to the smoke alarm and noticed the alarm system. *Hell!* She had forgotten. She continued to fan the smoke away from the alarm that was still squealing. The noise of ringing other than the alarm sounded out. She wheeled around to the door and realized the blazing sirens of the fire department had just pulled up at her house. Again!

She walked out of the house as the hotty firemen from the night before came barreling toward her with a hose in hand. "Never mind, boys, just burnt toast."

One stepped forward and took his helmet and mask off. A flash of perfect teeth greeted her with a wide grin.

*Ethan.*

The way the firemen were checking her out reminded Charly she was standing there in satin pajamas. What was it with her in pajamas and men in uniform? She was just thankful it wasn't her cloud ones, or her Mickey Mouse ones.

Her heart moved to her throat as the sexy Ethan winked.

"I burned toast," Chalry stammered, stunned by his good looks and thankful that his partners in flame fighting had not turned on the hose prior to approach. *I burned toast? Love a duck! I sound like an idiot.* She had already explained about the toast.

Ethan nodded and grinned. "You don't know how to make toast?"

"No," she told him, and tried to be calm. "I mean, yes, but the toaster..."

"It was the toaster's fault? Like it was the oven's last night?" Ethan stepped closer and his gaze searched her face.

Her cheeks started to sting — oh yeah, why not add to the no makeup, tossed hair, and pajama thing by blushing. "No, it was my fault. I just..."

"Wanted to see me again?" He lifted his brows.

"No, of course not." And her cheeks went from stinging to burning.

*This is not going well.*

"So you didn't want to see me again?" He

sounded so disappointed. "Yes, I wanted to see you..." Charly sighed in defeat. "Never mind." It was official; she was embarrassed.

Ethan chuckled, as did some of the guys behind him. Would it have been wrong of her to wish she could just evaporate and fade out like the clearing haze, the only remnant of the once tasty bread?

"You're a cutie." He turned to the guys behind him. "You might as well put the hose away. She doesn't need it."

There was something about her not needing a hose that put naughty thoughts in her head. The devil on her shoulder snickered, commenting about needing a hose all right. There was something about Ethan and his hose that held serious possibilities. The angel on the other side was preparing to retort.

"Look at this. I'm so glad to see young men in uniform." A voice rang out that was not the angel, but instead, the soul-saving elderly neighbor.

Looking at Mrs. Newman, Charly smiled. "Morning." She glanced to what appeared to be the much promised bundt cake.

*Oh good, more fat for my dimpling ass. Is there no mercy left in the world?*

Ethan smiled at the church going lady. "Hello, Mrs. Newman."

"Hello, Ethan, how's your mother? I'll be seeing her on Tuesday. We have a meeting for the society." She grinned and eyed him up in his coat and equipment.

"She's good," the sexy fireman offered. "I'll let her know you said hi."

"Such a good boy," Mrs. Newman fawned. "Your mother is so proud of you. Of course, not over the fact you haven't married."

"Well, uh..." Ethan stammered while his men chuckled.

"Wow! Welcoming committee, you really shouldn't have!" a familiar voice called.

Charly turned as Jenna approached from over by her truck. Charly hadn't even noticed her pull up.

*What is she doing here?* "Jenna?"

Her friend beamed and winked. "Indeed, I jumped in the truck and thought I'd surprise you."

"Oh, I'm surprised. There are hardly words." *She had to show up now?*

Jenna bounced her gaze between Ethan and Charly with sparkled amusement in her eye. "So, you did offer yourself up on a plate? I told you it would work!"

Charly's cheeks tinted again. Trust Jenna. "Jenna, this is Ethan." She pointed in the direction of the good-looking fireman with the killer smile. "And..."

"I'm Mrs. Newman, your friend's neighbor. I made a nice bundt cake." She passed it to Jenna.

"Oh, Charly!" a thick French accent called

as the sexy neighbor Jacque ran over from next door. He growled and grinned. "Looking like a scrumptious little strawberry tart this morning." He winked.

*Oh dear.*

Charly glanced at Ethan, who studied the other man in amusement. Jenna drooled over Jacque while Mrs. Newman watched everything going on with a strange little smile. "Morning, Jacque, how's the cooking?"

He winked and his dark gaze held mischief. Very sexy mischief. "I cook for you one night and satisfy your hunger."

*Right. I'm so short on dinner with men.* "That's sweet."

He grinned, then turned to Ethan. "I noticed your big truck." He eyed Ethan's uniform. "I need you to get your big ladder up and help with the pussy."

Jenna gasped. Charly's mouth parted, then closed in shock.

"I'm good at heating things up, but my ladder is short. Not so good for reaching the pussy." He tossed his hands in the air in frustration.

"I see." Charly's attention fell on Ethan. He looked as sexy as hell, despite the stunned expression he wore. The other men were covering their mouths and biting their lips from the chef's confessions

"You have a big ladder and help me? I love the pussy, but not always good with it.

63

No control." Jacque shrugged. "The pussy has a mind of its own."

A muffled snort forced Charly to glance at Jenna. She was dying to laugh and failing at the restraint.

"I don't think I'm understanding you." Ethan sounded as traumatized as the expression he wore on his gorgeous face.

"His cat," Mrs. Newman answered. "He needs help with Ambrose. She likes to get in tight places. What did you think he was talking about?"

A gasp left Charly. She looked to Ethan. His brows lifted and he grinned. He looked sinful. "I should go and rescue the cat." Ethan stepped back.

"I'm sure I'll see you soon." Charly's stomach fluttered out of control.

"I hope so." He moved toward Jacque and walked away with the crazy French chef.

Despite her recent supply of hot men, none of them affected her with a mere look like Ethan did. None of them had those eyes, or that smile. Sure, they were good-looking, but Ethan sizzled.

Turning to Mrs. Newman, Charly sighed. "Thank you for the cake. How have you been?"

Her face softened with a smile, accenting the lines that age had placed on her face. "I'm wonderful. I came to share a message that the

Lord has for you."

*Oh! This is fantastic.*

Jenna blinked. "Doesn't he usually put those messages on billboards?"

She didn't look at Jenna and continued to smile at Mrs. Newman. "And what did the Lord have to say to me today?" Charly couldn't believe she was encouraging this.

A thoughtful look dusted across the sweet elderly neighbor's features. "I just can't seem to remember offhand." She smiled warmly. "It'll come to me. It was like the other day."

"Oh, how so?"

"Well, I was in the grocery store looking at the produce section, trying to find avocadoes."

*And here we go.*

"I like avocadoes," Jenna agreed, not that Charly recalled Mrs. Newman asking.

"And I just didn't see any. Then I carried on with my shopping and there they were. They weren't in the produce aisle at all." Mrs. Newman nodded, beaming. "I tell you, those avocadoes were in the darndest place. Makes you wonder. They weren't where I was expecting them. I had to go through a few aisles before I turned and found them."

Charly blinked at her sweet elderly neighbor. Odd story, but the lady wasn't exactly young. No doubt a verse short of a Bible. "Imagine that." She thought on the avocado story.

"Well, take care, enjoy the bundt cake, and I'll visit you soon. My work here is done." She gave a wave. "Nice to meet you, Jenna. I hope to see you again."

"You too, thanks again for the cake." Jenna's gaze followed the departing church lady.

Her work here was done? She had said the same thing yesterday, or at least something similar.

The angel on Charly's shoulder whispered, *Maybe whatever Mrs. Newman had meant to tell you, she actually said.*

## Chapter Four

Charly had to admit to herself the evening spent with Jason had been fun and she wouldn't mind doing it again. Jenna had been able to babysit for her, which had been a relief on such short notice. Her friend informed her she would have Liz come over and keep her company. She could only imagine the conversation the two of them had and what new words had been introduced to Leigh's vocabulary.

Jason brought his BMW to a stop and turned off the ignition. He turned in his seat and smiled. "I had a really terrific time. Allow me to walk you up?"

She nodded and he opened the door, got out, and walked around to her door to open it. He certainly was a gentleman.

*Sweet, more points for the ball player.*

She stepped out of the car and he shut the vehicle door behind her.

They exchanged quick looks as they walked up her driveway and up the three small steps to the small porch at the front entrance. "I had an incredible time," he informed her while his gaze studied the details of her hair and face.

She smiled. "It was nice. Thank you. I should probably get in, though."

And there it was. The awkward and horrible first date jitters. The whole uncertain moment of, do I hug him? Do I kiss him? Do I let him do either? Wow, it had been a long time since she had been in this situation.

*What have I been doing with my time? Right, working and being a mom.*

Jason's green gaze dipped to her lips, then lifted.

*He is debating about kissing me. What the hell? He's good-looking and sexy. I'll take his lead.*

"So, this is good night?" she choked out, and debated reaching into her purse for her keys. Things had to move along; the anticipation was killing her.

He nodded and slipped his arms around her waist. Jason pulled her close, hard against his solid chest. "Thank you, Charly, you made a high school dream come true."

Tilting her head up, she couldn't help but be confused. "I didn't think you noticed me."

"Oh, I noticed you. It was true what I said at the doughnut shop yesterday. I've thought about you a lot. Always wondered what it would have been like to ask you out."

*Well I'll be damned. Men, even as teenage boys, don't make sense. Like that's a shock.*

His mouth curled into a grin and his brows lifted. Even under the faint glow of the porch light she could see amusement sparkle in his green catlike eyes. "You look surprised."

Charly nodded. "I guess I am."

His tongue moved across his lower lip slowly. He had great lips. "Then don't be surprised that I want to kiss you." His lips lowered toward her.

Her lashes fluttered closed and her heart raced. It was the moment she'd spent high school days fantasizing about. Jason's warm breath touched her face as his lips drew near their destination. The strength of the kiss as his lips pressed against hers was not knee-weakening like she thought it would be. She tried to move her lips, but his tongue had already moved into her mouth. Instead of the gentle exploring, desire reaching kiss that she was expecting, his tongue thrust deeper as if in search of her tonsils. If his tongue forced any further down her throat, the sexy baseball player was going to discover she didn't have any. Charly's lips became wet. Was that slobber, or did the hunk that had his arms around her just have a sloppy kiss? She tried to pull back, but her lips stuck as if the wetness had formed a vacuum seal.

*Is this the man of my teenage dreams, or a plunger attacking me?*

Panic filled Charly where longing should have been. She was going to suffocate, or drown. The latter was possible if her lips got any wetter. Maybe he was part dog and licking the flavored lip gloss off her lips like a kid with a lollipop. Both meant death.

*How terrifying, dying by the worst kiss in history.*

Finally, the near death experience ended as he lifted his lips. Stumbling back, she inhaled a sharp breath as if having experienced a traumatic event. Instinctively, Charly wanted to wipe her lips, as they had more liquid on them than if she had chugged back a large glass of milk. Come to think of it, she would have had less milk on her face than she currently had saliva.

Would the cool, night air chap her lips? And would it be overly rude to dry her face and reapply the lip gloss, in turn avoiding the dry, cracking sensation that a horrific event such as the one she had experienced could do to lips? Her lips were not accustomed to such elemental exposures.

"That was really great."

She smiled only because she struggled to choke back a laugh. *Great? What is he, a basset hound?* "I think I better get inside."

"I would love to do this again." His eyes locked with hers in anticipation.

*No! I'm a single mother; what if I'm not so lucky next time?* "Sounds like an idea." *Not a good one, but an idea nonetheless.*

What else could she say? The words, "oh yes, baby, lick my face like a wolf to pork chop" just seemed to fail to reach her lips. The lips that would need exfoliating and heavy moisturizer after that storm of...tongue?

Charly suppressed the defeated groan and smiled. "Good night, Jason. I had a great time."

_Until you kissed me._

"Good night, Charly."

She turned the knob to the front door and headed into the house, quickly shutting the door behind her and locking it. She leaned up against it,   thinking he might get the idea there was more lip gloss on her lips and want seconds. Sloppy seconds. That thought repulsed her. Jason was good-looking, but the worst kisser on earth.

"How was your date?" Liz asked as she and Jenna both turned to face her from their seats on the sofa.

"I need my toothbrush," Charly whined, and ran up the stairs. If she wasn't kissed again, it would be too soon.

Charly was happy to see Jenna and Liz. She was even happier that her date was over. She sat down on the sofa after she grabbed a glass from the kitchen and poured some wine.

"So, tell us about Jason. Jenna says he is hunkier now than in high school." Liz leaned forward in anticipation. Her green eyes danced.

"Hunkier,   yes.   However,   I   just experienced   the   ultimate   worst   kiss   in history." She sipped her wine and cringed at the mixed flavor it created with her freshly brushed teeth. "What were the two of you discussing?"

"Chris." Jenna smiled. "He's my friend with benefits."

"Like health care?" Jenna and Liz blinked at her. *What did I say so wrong?*

"No, Charly. Like a friend that you mutually agree to sleep with. You know, the no strings attached kind of thing?"

It was Charly's turn to blink. She stared disbelieving at Jenna.

Jenna rolled her eyes. "Chris and I have known each other for years, and since neither of us want a relationship, we have uncommitted, wild sex."

Liz turned to Jenna. "Now that Charly is here, tell us about the camera."

"A camera?" Charly sipped her wine.

Jenna nodded. "I still can't believe he brought a digital camera. I was like, 'what do you plan on taking a picture of?'"

"Gee, I wonder," Liz grunted with a giggle.

Jenna's eyes widened. "He reassured me he wouldn't take a picture of my face."

"At least the one above your shoulders," Liz laughed.

"Oh that's nice." *My friends are sex maniacs. I paint the naughty pictures. They just get to be naughty.*

"Needless to say, it didn't happen." Jenna tossed back the remainder of the wine in her glass. "Besides, who would actually let some guy take pictures of them?"

"You mean without being compensated?" Liz asked.

Charly tilted her head. "It's sad that we have to clarify such things."

"Well, the reason is because there was one time..." Liz started with an animated expression. She grabbed a chocolate from the box next to the wine and popped one in her mouth.

*Here we go, and the horror begins.*

"Oh! I love stories!" Jenna exclaimed. "Especially when they're stories of other people and not me."

"Imagine that." Charly snickered.

"That comment coming from a woman with a parade of half-naked and completely naked men and no recollection of what to do with them outside of a paintbrush and easel," Liz piped up with a mouth full of chocolate.

"Let's not talk about the painting." She was glad most days that her friends knew she was the infamous Joey Sinn. Other times, like now, it just sucked.

Jenna and Liz both looked at her. Their smiles were gone. "You still aren't painting?" Jenna exchanged a concerned look with Liz.

"The last thing I want to talk about is my painting, or shall I say, the lack thereof. I think that the whole incident with the stalker fan set me back."

"You need to have mind-blowing sex and clear your head," Liz told her like it was the cure to her lost muse.

Charly grimaced. "I don't think so."

"Well, she will certainly have lots of opportunity with two other offers for dinner," Jenna informed, like it was hers to share.

"Two dinner invitations? Wow, as in dates?" Liz choked on the sip of wine she took.

"Just swallow, then breathe," Jenna told her.

"You would think she would have that down by now," Charly added, then laughed.

Laughter left Jenna and Liz both. "So, who are your dates with?" Liz demanded.

"One should be good. The other—I almost committed her when I found out who the other was." Jenna was still not amused.

"Okay." Charly breathed in deep. "Jacque wants to cook dinner for me one night. Date of that is unknown."

"And?" Liz waited. "I don't think Jenna would commit you over dinner with that gorgeous French chef. Hell, he can bend me over in the kitchen and…"

"Officer Cole," Charly stated before Liz finished her comment. Knowing Liz, it would have been explicit.

*Hypocrite! You paint erotic pictures.* The

angel wasn't amused.

"Charly! How could you?"

"Liz, Jenna is exaggerating. It's not a date. It's a simple dinner to discuss my safety and a crazy fan."

Liz blinked. "Charly, how are you going to explain to Cole about a fan when no one other than Jenna and I know that you are Joey Sinn?"

*If I didn't have bad luck, I wouldn't have any.* "I never thought of that. Maybe he knows. I mean, New York did talk to him."

Jenna cleared her throat. "Charly, as I recall from your phone calls, they chalked it up as a stalker. Officer Skippy may have to be told your identity."

"Okay, Jenna said that you said he was hot, right?"

*Oh God, the world according to Liz.* "Yes. So?"

"Maybe you shouldn't lift brows if he's cute. Have sex with him; no relationship, though."

"I'm not looking for a relationship."

Jenna gasped. "Oh! Never say that, Charly. You might jinx yourself."

"But, then again, she might get laid," Liz laughed.

"Maybe." Charly smiled. "I think this is the most fun I've had in a while."

"It's not as much fun as sex," Liz chimed

in. "I remember this one time..."

"Save it for your memoirs," Jenna told her.

"Or as fun as kissing," Liz added, and took a sip of her wine.

"No, don't even go there. I'm still recovering from Jason." Charly rolled her eyes and looked at her friend. "You're the only one I know that has different categories for kissing."

"You don't?" Jenna was surprised.

It caught her off guard. "No, I take it you do too?"

Liz grinned. "See, you never listen to me. I think we've had that conversation more than once."

A strange ickiness fell over her. The devil on her shoulder laughed and commented about her lack of knowledge on kisses. *You better hope the topic of great sex doesn't come up,* he taunted. Even the angel seemed disappointed in her.

Her friends stared at her with looks of curiosity and worry. Liz shook her head as astonishment crossed her face. "Charly, do *not* tell me you haven't experienced the most delicious kiss of your life."

Charly frowned. "I've had some good kisses. In fact, I think I was good at it when I was younger."

"She said *great,* not good," Jenna clarified.

Charly looked to Liz, who cast a sarcastic little smile that turned into a snicker. "No great kisses?"

"I'm thinking."

Liz gasped. "No, Charly, if you have to think about it then you've never had one. Those head-cupping, heart-racing, toe-curling kisses that reach in and caress your soul as his lips graze yours. Where everything in the world around you fades out but that moment of time?"

"I love those kisses." Jenna sighed. A dreamy look softened her features.

The devil whispered something about being deprived. The angel wasn't speaking to her at all. That wasn't good sign.

"Apparently not," Charly breathed. *What have I missed out on?* The question was, would she ever experience it?

Charly's eyes snapped open. She was on her back in bed. She rolled her head to the alarm clock. Six fifteen in the morning. A Saturday morning, the day that most people slept in. The day they didn't have to drag their asses to the coffee pot and hover around it like a vulture over a dying body. Charly turned her head back and stared at the ceiling. "The bastard with the leaf blower is dying today."

She tossed back the expensive duvet and stomped to her bedroom door. With a quick tug and a turn of the knob, she pulled it open and all but ran down the stairs of her townhouse toward the living room. "The leaf-blowing, mow-your-lawn-at-stupid-hours-to-piss-you-off bastard is about to meet the redheaded devil." Yes, she was talking to herself in her frantic and pissed off state.Venting made her feel better. She pulled back the blinds and reached for the latch on the glass patio door. She stepped into the yard.

The fence that separated her and Jacque's yard was only five feet high. She was able to look over in his yard and noticed that the gorgeous French chef was grilling. Damn! It smelled good.

Taking thirty seconds longer than it should have, she realized the hunk with *cat* issues and a skillet on the grill wore nothing but an apron. A white apron, which tied at his waist. It exposed almost all of him and barely covered the *gourmet* between his legs in the front. Not that she could see the front, but she was an artist. She had imagination.

Her mood was far from pleasant and happy after being ripped from a dream that starred the delicious flame-fighting Ethan by a leaf-blowing maniac with a death wish. The fact she was coffee deprived didn't help.

Jacque had a fantastic butt and she, blessed by the morning sun, had a great view of every curve of tanned, tight buttocks. Of course, she also still had her bad luck. Jacque turned and smiled. "Morning, *chérie*, do you like what I have going?"

She was unclear if he was referring to his fantastic assets, since in addition to his tight and damn near perfect butt, his back was strong and his shoulders broad, or if he was talking about what he was cooking. "It smells wonderful."

He wiggled his brows and took in her satin pajamas. Apparently, her knack for showing up in front of gorgeous men in sleepwear wasn't reserved for those in uniform, it was for those even out of all clothes.. An apron didn't constitute an outfit. It barely categorized as a loincloth. However, Jacque wore it well. Now, if he would only be so kind to peel her a grape.

"You must wonder about my nakedness."

*Nope, not wondering. Strictly appreciating at this time.*

He nodded as if he understood. "I like to have freedom when I create scrumptious things for the taste buds. I like to release inhibitions." He stepped away from the large gas grill, closer to the fence and her.

Yep, the apron covered. It was almost a disappointment, but not as much as the fact that the man with long dark hair wasn't holding grapes. She then remembered the comment he had made the day before about his short ladder and was curious; what woman wouldn't be?

"There's nothing worse than a cook with inhibitions. Nakedness throws mine away." He emphasized his point with the wave of a metal flipper.

"Well, good for you," she answered before thinking. She'd tossed all verbal thought to the wind. The same wind that teased at the hem of his apron. The lack of caffeine was her only defense.

He sighed in a whimsical, almost dreamy sort of way then winked jet black lashes at her. "I still cook for you, my strawberry tart. You and the little cookie cruncher."

She sighed. "I appreciate the offer, but…"

He rolled his eyes and a playful groan escaped his lips. "*Chérie*, you need not worry about me. I don't come onto you."

Charly frowned. *Oh dear, where is this going?*

"I not that kind."

Suddenly, she was confused. Maybe she misunderstood his broken English. "What kind?"

*You look very male to me.*

"I don't mess with another man's dessert."

Charly shook her head. "Oh, Jason? No, my date last night was just that. It was a date." She sighed and remembered the kiss from hell then fought the urge to wince and keep stomach bile at bay.

"I see, not a good date?"

"No, good date, great even, then a horrible kiss." She was stunned at her bluntness. Her hand flew to her mouth. "I can't believe I said that."

"I won't tell, but bad kiss is well worse than frozen food." He glanced over to the grill then back at her. "It was not the BMW man I was thinking of when I said about another man's dessert."

Charly adored Jacque already. "Trust me, there are no other men in my life. Actually, Jacque, there are, but..."

He winked again and grinned. "I cook for you in my nakedness as friends."

She sighed and thought a moment. "Would you let me paint you?"

"An artist?" He grinned. "I will get naked for you whenever and wherever you need, providing he will not mind so much."

Confused, Charly shook her head. "Really, I'm not involved."

A puzzled look crossed the well-built and sexy chef's face. "I just thought that you might be with the cherries jubilee. He looked like you were his favorite topping, no?"

She frowned. Nope, there were no cherries in her life. Especially cherries that were on fire. Realization dawned on her. "You mean Ethan, the fireman?" She sighed. "I think he's the only man that hasn't asked me to dinner."

"Aww, *chérie*." He tilted his head to the side and donned an understanding expression. "No need to look like there's not enough whipped cream. Make a move."

She frowned and didn't understand. "Move what?"

A hearty chuckle escaped Jacque's firm lips. "Let him know he's *your* favorite dish."

Charly glanced around the edible chef to the smoke at the grill. "Jacque, you might want to check your breakfast."

He turned. "Ah, gotta go, *chérie*. Think what I said. We have snacks soon; kiss the cookie cruncher for me."

"Will do." Charly studied the movement of Jacque's muscles and butt as he hurried over to the grill. *Now that is art in the making.* With all the eye candy at her disposal, why was she having such a hard time painting?

The sound of the leaf blower pulled her attention from the edible chef who scooped stuff of the large, expensive barbeque and hurried through his patio doors. The loud, obnoxious, impossible-to-think-over-the-noise leaf blower grew louder. The man was about to die. She stepped forward and waited. Large, broad, and bare shoulders stepped into view.

"What the hell are you doing?" she barked.

The leaf blower stopped. The shoulders turned, revealing a solid chest and ripped abs. She pulled her gaze from the carved body so defined and in amazing shape she swore each muscle had been hand carved and glanced up into dark brown eyes.

"Wow! Ms. Jamieson. You're even more beautiful than what they said."

Blinking, Charly took in the details of the man's handsome face. Again, a completely gorgeous man with a delightful body was standing in front of her. What was it doing, raining men?

*"It never rains, but it pours."* Mrs. Newman's words echoed in her mind. That was it. Charly needed coffee and to stop wondering if she had been cursed by the church lady. Maybe that was a contradiction, but nonetheless…

"I hope I didn't wake you, Mrs. Jamieson."

*Speak, don't be dumbfounded. He maybe a hunk with nice eyes, but they're not as nice as Ethan's are.* She chastised the devil on her shoulder. The bastard had too much opinion.

"You did, actually, yesterday and today. Now who the hell are you?"

He smiled.

*Son of a bitch, very sexy. I'm not noticing.* It was lie, but if you couldn't lie to yourself, who could you lie to?

83

*Everyone you meet*, the angel piped up. Sure, the voice of reason. She needed to get meds.

"I'm an early riser. I can't help myself, but I love a good blowjob. I insist on it daily." His mouth curled into a broad grin and she waited for stars and satellites to fall from the sky from the impact.

The lack of caffeine had officially killed brain cells. After a comment like that from the hunk in front of her, not only did her thoughts have nothing to do with leaves, but also she wondered about the man's *ladder*. "What?"

He chuckled. "I'm Raul, the gardener." He extended a hand and by some miracle or work of God, she shook it out of politeness.

"I'm Charly. Ms. Jamieson was my former mother-in-law and a first class bitch."

His brows lifted. "I understand." His gaze raked over her pajamas. "Well, Charly, I must say that you have the nicest buds on the block."

Now what the hell? "Come again?"

"Your rose bushes." He looked to one of the shrubs in her yard.

It was the end of January, they weren't blooming, and she was lucky to keep a houseplant alive. How was she to know? "I didn't realize they were roses."

He nodded once. "I can help you with your flowerbed. I know all about buds and how the petals should be treated."

*Why is my mind stuck in the gutter? Jenna and Liz are a real bad influence.*

*Says the woman who paints scandalous sin.* The devil on her shoulder was a cynic at best. *Oh sure, blame your friends. Take no accountability for your actions,* the angel protested in disgust.

"I can come regularly."

Charly snapped back to the moment and lifted her brows. "I'm sorry, could you please repeat that?"

He flashed another killer smile. "I said I can come regularly, as often as you need."

*Oh! I need all right.*

"What a nice offer." What else could she say? Though she started to wonder on her sanity at this point. What was going on?

He pushed open the small gate and stepped in to the ten-foot by ten-foot yard. "You're sweet and beautiful." He glanced to the flowerbed with the rosebush then rested his attention back on her. "When I found out from the association a woman had bought the place, I was surprised. Mrs. Newman has been the only woman on this street for years. She's an interesting lady."

"That she is," Charly agreed with a smile. "She sure loves to bake."

"That she does, but she's a wise one. I guess age does that." He stepped closer and locked his gaze with hers. "You're a totally different kind of woman." His voice was low and sexy.

Her heart picked up a bit of speed from the sexy gardener's proximity as well as the sparkle in his eye that match the tone of his voice. She was a businesswoman and could handle this. Maybe. "I know nothing about flowers."

He waved a hand, indicating not to worry. She was positive every perfectly defined muscle moved from his shoulder to his abs. "I have no problem giving yours special attention. I'd love to come in your garden."

*Is it me, or do the innuendos just keep coming?*

"I should go make coffee." *And call a shrink.* She pointed to the patio door, which would take her back inside to the safety of her house and away from men with pick-up lines and whatnot in abundance.

"You're beautiful." Raul's eyes caressed her features as she stared into his dark brown eyes. His gaze fell to her lips as his hand gently caressed underneath her chin.

*Who needs coffee or lucid thought? Both are highly overrated.*

Slowly, he tilted her face up as his head lowered toward her. His long, dark lashes fluttered closed. She closed her eyes as his warm, soft lips touched hers.

Her heart pounded in her chest and echoed into her ears as she parted her lips to take in a breath. His tongue touched her lower lip softly and she waited... The kiss was nice, warm, and tender. It was a good kiss, but...nothing happened.

The kiss was ordinary, bordering on bland. Where were the fireworks? The bells and whistles never came. Her toes were far from curling. Again, an incredibly good-looking man had kissed her and yet, she had been deprived of the soul-searing passion that a great kiss supposedly possessed. She had been disillusioned by the building of the moment, reeled in by the anticipation and, in the end, disappointed.

Raul pulled his lips from hers suddenly and she opened her eyes. He stared into her eyes and he frowned. "I knew it."

She was unsure as to what the hunky gardener was referring. "Knew what?"

He smiled weakly. "I had to kiss you to make sure."

"Make sure of what?" Charly hoped that he wasn't going to tell her that it was the best kiss of his life.

"I know this is going to sound strange." He looked unsure, hesitant even.

*Oh no! Mayday!* the angel on her one shoulder cried in panic. *This should be good,* the devil on the other side laughed.

"You are so beautiful, Charly, that I had to confirm it."

Raul, despite his gorgeous appearance and mythological godlike body, was making her nervous. "Confirm what?" Did she miss something?

Raul nodded. "I've wondered for some time, and kissing you proved it."

Charly blinked in disbelief. She needed to stop interacting with people before she had consumed caffeine. "I'm sorry, what did you need to prove?"

"I'm gay."

*I'm officially skipping coffee and having tequila. It's going to be one of those days.*

## Chapter Five

After her more than eventful morning, Charly made coffee, sent Leigh off shopping with Liz, and power tidied the house. It was clean, and now she had time on her hands. Between the bad kiss with Jason the night before, and then having Raul kiss her and tell her he was gay, her confidence was totally shattered. Men were stupid, except for Jacque. The sexy but eccentric chef's words about Ethan looking interested had her mind going. Not that she should venture into those fires with her track record over the last twenty-four hours, but there was just something about Ethan.

Some good came from Ethan thoughts. She was motivated to haul out her easel and some paints and hang out in her garden. Painting was a constructive distraction from the hot fireman. She shouldn't be thinking about him. It didn't matter how sexy he was; something would just go wrong. She blinked at the canvas and stared into amazing blue eyes. "Bastard!" How dare he rule her paintbrush like that? Just like a man to move in and takeover, even if it was her stuck-in-the-gutter mind to blame. "On the bright side, I didn't paint your, err, ladder?"

*You've never even seen his ladder,* the devil mocked. *Think pure thoughts,* the angel scolded. At that moment, Charly was sure that the devil on her one shoulder had knocked the angel out because it wasn't the ladder she thought about. It was the fact she needed the hose.

Her mind danced images of Ethan in her mind. Slowly undressing, he took off his shirt. Her nipples tightened at the thought of a tanned, perfectly sculpted chest and defined abdomen. His hands slid to the buckle of his jeans. Oh yeah, this was a daydream. The sound of the front doorbell chimed.

"Whoever is on my step is dead." Placing her paint pallet down, she walked to the front door and tore it open. She blinked in disbelief with a fleeting ounce of guilt.

*Oh hell!* "Mrs. Newman, what a wonderful surprise."

"Good morning, Charly. God has blessed us with a beautiful day, hasn't he?"

*Up until you rang my bell.* "Indeed. What can I do for you?"

"This morning, when I was making tea, the Lord wanted me to give you a message."

*Double hell!*

"Only, I got busy going through my storage closet and I forgot. However, I found this book for your daughter. It was one of my daughter's favorites until she grew up and married one of Satan's own and he moved her away from me to an entirely different state."

*Wow! She sounds hostile. So, the church lady has a story and anger issues.* Charly took the book and smiled. "That's very thoughtful. Thank you, Leigh will love it."

"Yes, it's about a princess that kisses frogs. She thinks one day that she should just give up, that the fairy Godmother was wrong and she would never find her prince. Then she kisses one last frog and presto!"

*She got a wart.*

Mrs. Newman smiled. "She found Prince Charming."

The slam of car door sounded. Charly and Mrs. Newman both turned to the parked vehicle. Her heart slammed to a stop and her stomach fluttered out of control. The breath she had inhaled stuck in her throat. He was in a blue golf shirt the same color as his eyes and it tucked into a fitted pair of well-worn jeans. The man was sin, or at least cause her to commit a few. "Hello, ladies," his sexy rumble greeted. The timbre of his voice dampened her thong immediately.

"Ethan, what a delightful surprise!" Mrs. Newman greeted.

"Hello." Ethan smiled at the elderly woman, and then turned to Charly. "Hi."

"Hi." They just stood there and stared at each other. In record time, she found herself lost in his blue gaze.

"Well, I must be going," Mrs. Newman informed them with a hint of humor in her voice.

Charly broke the eye lock and turned. "Thank you for stopping by, and for the book. I know Leigh will love it." She collected her thoughts and ignored her heart thumping a lot faster than it had been before Ethan's arrival. "I will be sure to send Leigh over and thank you personally when she gets home."

She smiled sweetly. "That will be lovely, dear."

"Oh, Mrs. Newman, the reason I stopped by. My mom wanted me to give you these. Something about your meeting on Tuesday." Ethan passed her sweet neighbor the papers in his hand.

"Thank you, Ethan. You kids have a nice chat."

"Actually, Mrs. Newman." She remembered the light in the kitchen. "I need the number of that handyman you get. My kitchen light is broken. I'm sure it's the switch."

"I wouldn't want you to spend the money when I'm here and can look at it."

Ethan's words surprised her. "I, err, yes, thank you. I mean, if I'm not keeping you from something."

"There you go," Mrs. Newman, gushed with a little more happiness than usual. "Bye, kids, have a nice time." She hurried off at a record speed. Charly didn't even know the little old lady could move that fast.

Ethan waved to Mrs. Newman then turned back. "I really don't mind. A single mom raised me." A small smile tugged his lips and unexpectedly, she became slightly mesmerized by his smile. "I learned how to do a lot of things to help my mom out so she wasn't calling people over simple stuff."

Charly studied the man before her and knew immediately he wasn't just a gorgeous face. She suspected he might be a really nice guy too. Charly also doubted she could be that lucky. "I would appreciate it."

"I'd like to be able to help you with the light and anything else you might need."

*I need your hose.* "How sweet, come on in. It's the main light in the kitchen."

She stepped into the house and he followed. The faint scent of his cologne reached her nose and infiltrated her lungs with a shallow breath. There was something wonderful about the woodsy aroma mixing with manly soap and male. Her senses went on alert. Ethan was purely male. He shut the door behind him and glanced around.

"It's here." She flipped the light switch on and off. "I don't think it's the bulb, but I don't have a ladder."

"I'm tall enough I don't need a ladder if I can stand on one of your kitchen chairs." He closed the distance between them and smiled.

She tried to breathe. This close to him, seeing, smelling, and dreaming of tasting him made it hard. "I don't mind." *Hell, you can bend me over it, or you can sit and I'll straddle you, or we could forget the chair altogether.* "There's the table if you so feel the need."

His full lips parted and his tongue danced across his lower lip. "I'll keep it in mind."

She needed to turn the heat down because it was now sweltering in the house.

"We'll start with the chair."

*I could only wish.*

She walked to the table and pulled out a heavy oak chair out then slid it over to where he stood. His gaze never left her and the temperature of the room increased. "One chair."

"Thanks, do you have a tool kit?"

*Which one? The one with my vibrator or the one with hammer?*

"Let me get it." She stepped around him to the closet and decided not to get the one from her dresser drawer. Ethan got up on the chair. He had his back to her, giving Charly the most incredible view of his butt. He was denim delicious from where she stood.

Charly turned and ducked back into the closet. She didn't need him seeing her appraise his great butt as if it was artwork.

Not that she couldn't turn it into a piece of art. Getting Ethan the fireman naked would be ideal. Once naked, she would want sex. Looking at him in clothes made her want to have sex with him. Ethan naked? Her thong dampened further. At this rate, it would be soaked by the time he left.

"Do you need help?" his sexy baritone asked as she wrapped her hand around the handle of the metal box.

*Yes, just take my thong now.*

"I'm good." She closed the closet door and set the tool kit on the kitchen counter. His eyes were on her, Charly sensed it. Her skin flamed. "What did you need?"

"Something for a screw."

*Take me.*

She spun and blinked at him. He winced and smiled. "A screwdriver is what I meant."

"Of course." She opened the toolbox and her cheeks heated. She exhaled. "What kind?"

"A long one."

*No wicked thoughts,* the angel warned in a scolding tone. The only remark from the devil on her other shoulder was a sinister chuckle. Oh that couldn't be good.

An image of her straddling Ethan, licking his chest, came to mind. Too late on not having wicked thoughts. She picked up a bunch of screwdrivers and faced him. "You choose."

He frowned and cast a quizzical stare. "You look flushed; are you okay?"

"Warm." *Too warm for sanity and it has everything to do with you.*

Ethan smiled and narrowed his deep blue gaze. "Do you need help with your thermostat?"

*Lord, have mercy.*

"I can easily check that out once I flip your switch." His eyes widened and his lips parted. "I mean, the light switch."

"Right." Okay, maybe she wasn't delusional, which, being creative, always held out as a possibility. Maybe, just maybe, he too experienced the attraction.

A strange expression etched itself into his handsome face. "Would I be able to get an ice water?"

Dollars to doughnuts, he was equally as attracted to her, but she was so long out of the dating and courting game, she couldn't be sure. "Absolutely, I'll have one with you." She was losing her mind. Nope, she had lost it somewhere between the chemical reaction she was having to him and her wet lace excuse for underwear.

She had seen more naked men than there were flavors of Jelly Bellies—which were at least fifty regular flavors, not including seasonal and special editions—and she was acting like a virgin. Charly walked to the cupboard and grabbed out two tall glasses, then retrieved the ice from the freezer. How the ice cubes didn't melt in her fingers when they touched her skin was a miracle — and a half. With a deep inhale of her lungs, in hope to calm her sex drive, she put the frozen plastic block tray back in the freezer and poured the water into the glasses. She turned and took in the front of him on the chair with his arms up. Her eyes fell on the zipper of his jeans. The fireman appeared to have a good-sized *ladder* indeed

*If only he were naked on my bed.*

"Can you give me a hand?"

"With what?" She snapped her eyes up to his gaze.

"I need you to hold my globe." His lashes slammed shut and he most definitely winced that time. He shook his head then opened his eyes and smiled.

*Is that embarrassment on his handsome face?*

"I need you to hold the cover for the light." He snapped his fingers and grinned, though the sparkle didn't quite reach his eyes. "Never mind, I think I'll take that ice water now." He climbed down and set the globe on the counter as Charly cringed at the dust on its soft white surface. Martha Stewart she was not.

Ethan picked up one of the glasses of water.

Part of her was appalled at the dust, and a sick sense of embarrassment numbed her for a fleeting second. "I should probably run something over that."

The sexy man's eyes widened. "Over what?"

*Do not be a blatant hussy!* the angel practically screamed. *She needs to reach for the ladder,* the devil suggested with a chuckle.

*I'm going to hell. Thank Christ it'll be in a designer handbag. Oh God! Now I sound like Liz. I'm doomed.*

"It's dirty." Her voice left in a whisper as she pointed to the dust-covered object.

His very kissable lips parted as he turned to the glass he'd removed from the light. He glanced back to her. His blue eyes were almost navy now in color. "You might as well run something over it while it's in your reach."

*Was that an invite?*

Charly's mouth went dry. She picked up the other glass, the one she'd poured for herself. "How's the water?"

"Very cold. It's perfect, thank you." He downed the water and set the glass in the sink.

"Anything else you need?" She sipped the water.

A strange and unreadable expression dusted across his features for a fleeting moment before he cast a lopsided grin. "I better hurry up and get this done. Then you can get back to what you were doing."

*Trying not to think of you.* That was shot to hell now, wasn't it? "You're not keeping me from anything. I appreciate this." She genuinely meant the words. After all, she was an artist not an electrician.

His blues regained the sparkle. "I'm glad I could help, anytime."

*Wonderful, how's ten o'clock? Say, my bedroom, you naked.* "I'll keep it in mind."

His lips twitched into a smile. "I hope so." They stood there staring at each other. He finally stepped back over to the chair, climbed up, and adjusted something with the screwdriver. "Can you flip the switch for me?"

Charly walked over to the plastic seesaw embedded on the wall and pushed it up. The light came on. "Incredible."

He chuckled. Her body tingled from the sound and she silently swore that she was going to climax right there. She walked to the counter and grabbed a damp cloth for the light cover.

He climbed down off the chair and his steps neared her. "It was easy. I'm good with my hands."

"I bet you are." She dropped the cover in the sink and it shattered. She turned and looked at him.

"You didn't cut yourself, did you?" His hand reached for hers. Heat shot through her body.

"I'm fine. What I meant was—" *What did I mean?* His gaze lowered to her lips, then lifted and met hers.

"I know what you meant." His head lowered slightly to hers. Her lashes fluttered closed. His breath caressed her skin.

The front door flung open. "We're back from shopping!" Liz called out.

Ethan released her hand and stepped back. Charly turned as her daughter rushed in. "You're the fireman."

Ethan glanced at Leigh then to the object in her hand. "Hi, sweetie, what do you have?"

She held up a stuffed pink pig. "My aunt got it for me. I'm calling him Paintbrush."

"I think that's a great name."

Her daughter's face turned animated and, for the first time in months, looked genuinely happy as she stared up at Ethan. "Really? You like the name?"

He nodded and winked. "I do."

Charly's heart tugged and she wondered if maybe her daughter was missing out on something. Probably not. She had Charly, Jenna, and Liz—not to mention Mrs. Newman—at her eight-year-old disposal.

Liz walked over to the sink and studied the broken glass light cover before lifting her gaze. "I'm not going to ask. Just go get ready for your date. Officer Skippy will be here soon."

Charly winced. *Thanks for the reminder, mood-wrecker.*

Her friend glanced over her shoulder at Ethan, then shot Charly a blanching look. Liz's back was to Ethan and she mouthed, *"Sorry."*

"I was just leaving," Ethan announced, and walked toward the door.

*No!* Charly turned to Ethan and her heart sank. "Thank you for your help."

He smiled and nodded then crossed the threshold and shut the door behind him. She turned to Liz. "If you weren't my best friend, I think I'd kill you."

Her friend bounced her gaze between Charly and the now empty entryway. "That man is gorgeous. Who is he?"

"The fireman," Leigh answered. "He came to put out Mommy's fire."

Charly sighed and sunk her teeth into her tongue.

*Mommy could only wish.*

Charly walked in her front door, shut it tight, and locked the bolt. She wondered where she had seriously gone wrong with officer Scepetti as she leaned against the heavy metal blocking the outside world and her disastrous night. Her life had just officially taken a turn for the unusual, yet again. She replayed the evening's events and groaned out loud. She wanted to throw up. No, she wanted ice cream and to get so drunk that she would forget everything. Since Alzheimer's wasn't in her immediate future, or one of those zappy things like in the movies that erased memories, ice cream and wine were the next best things.

She wanted to block the images of her most recent catastrophe of a date. Acting like a masochistic individual, she carried around the heavy weight on her chest. The man she wanted didn't want her. *Ethan!* Her heart tightened at the thought of his gorgeous smile and startling blue gaze that had held her no less than mesmerized more than once.

Frustrated, and certain she had just bruised the ego of Skippy the wonder cop beyond repair, she sulked. Sad thing was, she liked Cole. Just not enough to marry him, under any arrangements. "It's not my fault he fell in lust with me," she protested to her Gucci handbag, then proceeded to toss it to the floor by Leigh's backpack.

She stepped into the living room and halted. She blinked and trauma settled over her. "What the hell?"

The sight before her unfolded and her brain digested the unexpected. Jason removed his body off Liz, breaking their intense lip lock. Liz pulled down her shirt and Charly's mouth dropped open. Jason, the sexy but bad kisser ball player was making out with her best friend on a five thousand dollar leather sofa. Her sofa.

"Charly!" Liz gasped, sitting up. "You're way earlier than I planned on." A confused expression crossed her face. "What are you doing home?"

Looking to Jason, Charly held off on an answer. "Hi, Jason."

He sighed, looked guilty, then shifted and stood from the sofa. "Charly, about us. I got thinking all today and, though I had a great time with you last night, I know you're not the one."

"What one?" *Bad night here, people. Spell it out as if I were a three-year-old.*

"The one as in, I think we'd make better friends." He winced, and she was positive he held his breath.

*The "just friends" line is worse than your kiss, but better than you telling me you're gay.* "Unbelievable." This was the worst night of her life. Alcohol and calories were her only escape from this travesty of an existence. Tomorrow had to be better.

At a loss for words or even a quick comeback, she stepped into the kitchen and opened the freezer door. She needed the remedy for this hellish misery and she knew just the cure. Who the hell did Ethan think he was walking away from her? What the hell was Cole thinking? That he could just sail into her life and think she would love him after he had failed so miserably as a law enforcer?

*Men!*

Charly didn't see the pint of the chocolate caramel pecan ice cream that she knew was in there. She had it on reserve for moments like this. Her frustration level rose and she moved the three bags of French fries out of the way.

*No chocolate caramel pecan ice cream. What the hell?*

She knew it was there and moved the other frozen items in her path to the back of the fridge, out of her way.

Finally, she found the item she had been in desperate search of and wrapped her hand around its small, round cardboard container. Liz and Jason walked into the kitchen.

"What are you doing?" Liz asked as Charly pulled her head out of the freezer.

She clutched the pint of ice cream in a death grip. "Sulking!" she snapped, holding the pint close to her heart in a protective fashion.

"Charly, I really didn't think you would take this so hard. I'm really sorry."

"Get over yourself, Jason." She all but snapped at him—still traumatized from the scene on her couch. "I'm not sulking about you. Friends is fine!"

Liz glanced around at the kitchen floor and then back up at Charly. "Really? You could have fooled me."

Charly glanced to the floor, realizing that in her hunt down of her life's latest addiction, the contents of the freezer that had gotten in her way now lay on the kitchen floor and counter like beached whales.

Scowling, she headed over to the drawer that held the cutlery, pulled it open, and took out a spoon. "I had a bad date. A living hell, actually. Anything and everything that could have possibly gone wrong did. I realized that things were not good when I started hoping partway through the main course at dinner that I would get abducted by aliens in order to put me out of my misery."

"Wow, bad night, huh?" Jason started to pick up the strewn contents and repack the freezer.

Charly took the lid off the ice cream and peeled back the safety seal, then plunged her spoon into the chocolaty depths. Her mouth watered, knowing that she was going to be giving in to pure, unadulterated calories. "Cole asked me to marry him," she blurted out, then silenced herself by cramming a well-heaped spoon of chocolate, nuts, and more chocolate into her mouth.

"A marriage proposal?" Jason slammed the now repacked freezer door and stared with wide eyes.

Liz gasped and Jason stepped to her side.

"Skippy wants to marry you?" Liz shook her head and waved her hand as if to say, "enough."

"What did you say?" Jason's brows lifted. "Liz told me the story about when you moved in." He wasn't happy with the officer, that was obvious.

Charly swallowed another mouthful of tender morsels of ice cream.

*He needs to ask?* "I told him that nothing in the world would make me happier and I would get right on that after I poked my eyes out with pencils and dumped acid in my ears."

Liz frowned at her overwhelming sarcasm. "So you said no, right? Some things need to be clarified, damn it."

Charly groaned. "He thought that he would get his promotion faster if he was married. I, of course, would be safe, married to a cop. A marriage of convenience, can you believe it? Aren't really uber cheesy romances based on that kind of thing?"

"Yes, sadly." Liz blinked and turned to Jason. "The police department does drug testing, right?"

Jason nodded. "Yes, but my guess is the cop should be double checked." They both turned back to her.

Groaning, she set the ice cream and spoon onto the counter and scurried over to the fridge for the bottle of wine she knew was chilling. It was a big bottle of wine, but it had a glass out of it already, so at least she didn't have to fight with the cork. "I can't believe you think I would actually say yes to him. I'm completely crazy about someone else." She paused and glanced to the sexy ball player. "And for the record, Jason, it's not you."

Liz blanched. "So, what you're saying is you're still upset at me for interrupting the almost kiss between you and Ethan earlier?"

"He just walked away. Like I was invisible."

"He's insane," Jason assured her. "You are far from invisible, Charly!"

She glared at the hunky in her kitchen and pouted then pulled the cork out of the bottle. Charly took a healthy sip out of it, thinking at this point a glass would only slow her down. "You gave me the 'just friends' line," she confessed, and her eyes pricked with the threat of tears.

*Oh yeah, I have makeup on, which means I'll resemble a raccoon if I actually cry.*

She took another swig out of the wine bottle.

*Classy,* the angel grunted in sarcastic disgust. *Keep going, baby, life is hell,* the devil encouraged.

Jason's face scrunched. "How did the cop take the news of you saying no?"

"I wouldn't be surprised if the man is currently hanging himself, or at the very least, getting the rope to do it." At least she was honest and still not full of enough calories or wine.

"Oh, he took it that well." Liz's eyes widened. "Not good."

"Actually, turning him down was not the highlight of the evening." She stepped back over to the ice cream. With the hand not gripped around the wine bottle like life support, she removed the spoon still jabbed in the pint then plunged back into the ice cream.

Liz laughed. "I find that a hard one to top."

"Well..." She thought of the horrible event that followed her rejection of Cole's proposal and shoved more ice cream in her mouth. She could still see things too clearly. "I managed to awe myself with the unfortunate circumstances that followed." Maybe she shouldn't talk with a mouthful of frozen milk and chocolate, but this was a desperate moment in time.

"Unfortunate circumstances?" Jason's tone revealed his uncertainty and he studied her with a concerned expression.

"Oh yes," Charly admitted, taking the wine and washing down the ice cream with another large sip. She stared at the hunky ball player, obviously very much into Liz.

"What did you do?" Liz panicked, then stopped. "I'm not bailing you out, so you obviously didn't inflict bodily harm on the heart-shattered Skippy."

"Well, you know, he thought he would be all sweet and romantic and pulled me next to that incredibly muscled chest to hold me tight."

"He does have a nice chest; I'll give him that." Liz turned to Jason. "Yours is better."

Seriously? This was really happening? She glared at Liz. "Can we focus?"

"Forgive me if I am not feeling overly sorry for you." Her friend laughed.

"Oh, but do you think the evening of horrors could stop there?" Charly crammed more ice cream in her mouth, followed by the wine chaser. She swallowed. "No, he had to kiss me. Yes, he actually brought his lips to mine in a good kiss, after whispering the words 'I will change your mind' into my ear."

Jason snorted. "Not smart, but that takes a lot for a guy. Turning down his marriage proposal, no matter the reason...you can't hurt a male ego worse than that."

Halting from her wine and ice cream binging, she stared at them. "Apparently, I can."

"What did you do to Skippy?"

She darted a scowl at Liz. "Careful, you almost sound sorry for him."

Her friend since high school shook her head and furrowed her brows. "I'm thinking maybe I have a reason."

Charly nodded sadly. "Boy, do you ever. You see, I not only turned down the sexy officer's offer of marriage…I murmured Ethan's name during the kiss."

Jason winced, and then groaned. "Oh, you didn't?"

"Oh, but I did."

He stepped forward and wrapped her in a hug. "Okay, sweetheart, I would say that's a bad night." Jason eased back. "I think you should talk to this Ethan."

Her friend nodded in agreement. "He's right. Tell him that your date was a nightmare and that you want to go out with him."

Were they both nuts? "As in ask him out on a date?"

Chuckling, Jason stepped back over next to Liz. "I would say it's a start, unless you have a better idea?"

She debated a moment. "Yes, more wine and ice cream." Charly reached for the spoon as Jason and Liz exchanged a worried glance.

Ethan Valiant stared out the bay door of the fire station at the rain coming down. His eyes rested on the empty shop space that would soon house the city's new art gallery. Charly's art gallery. He pouted, and for the umpteenth time, knew he should have kissed her yesterday. Maybe she would have forgotten about her date with Cole. He sighed as the police car pulled up and Cole jumped out. "Hey, Ethan."

*Well, if it isn't the devil himself.* "Hi, Cole, what's up?" Despite being friends a while, he couldn't help but be less than enthusiastic to see the other man.

"I wanted to talk to you about something when you have a minute."

"No alarms going off; I'm available now."

*Be nice, it's not his fault he beat you in asking her out. You should've opened your mouth and said something instead of thinking how beautiful she was.*

"Charly, the lady with—"

"I know who she is."

"Right. Well, her gallery is opening up across the street and, since it's across from the station, I thought maybe you and the guys could keep an eye on it."

*Odd request.* "Is there a problem?"

Cole hesitated. "Actually, there is. She moved here from New York to get away from a hell-bent stalker. She's still a little scared and I thought you might be a good person to help her out."

"Me?" Ethan was stunned. "Why me?" *You went on the date with her. You're also the cop, the cop who didn't take the stalker seriously, if I remember correctly.*

Sighing, Cole glanced around. "I think she likes you."

"I heard from her friend that you went to dinner with her last night." *I sound jealous. Hell, I am.*

111

"I did. That's why I know she likes you... A lot."

Curious, Ethan tilted his head and stared at Cole. "She didn't actually come out and say it, did she?"

"No, she's much too ladylike for that. Only, I ended up kissing her."

*I didn't need that information.*

Cole hesitated and he winced. "She murmured your name."

Slapping a hand to his mouth, Ethan wanted to laugh. Instead, he covered his grin. *Don't revel.* He forced his smile down and lowered his hand. "That's rough."

Cole chuckled. "Rough is an understatement. I remembered the night I first met her and the way you two looked at each other."

He normally didn't rejoice in his friends or anyone's misfortunes, but this time was totally different. "She seems nice."

"She's great." His gaze narrowed. "I think there's more to that stalker thing. No one in New York will talk about it. It was pretty bad, though, threatening. I have the file and will go over it tonight. They were concerned back east and I guess that's why I'm worried."

Ethan didn't like the sound of that. "I'll let the guys know to not say anything, but have them keep an eye out."

"That would be good." Cole smiled then tilted his head and studied Ethan. "You like her, don't you?"

"Yeah, from the moment I saw her. As cheesy and romantic as that sounds," Ethan admitted. "I think even my mom would like her."

Groaning, Cole laughed. "That would be a first for you."

"Tell me about it." Ethan banished all thoughts of his mother and every other woman he had dated. He'd stopped dating altogether two years ago. He had avoided women like the plague. Now, he didn't want to avoid one.

His friend grinned and lifted his brows. "She's at the gallery now, but you didn't hear it from me." Cole turned and walked away. "Call me. We'll go for a beer."

Ethan grinned. "I will." His smile faltered. "If you find anything else about that situation in New York, let me know."

Cole opened the car door and nodded. He got in the police cruiser and pulled away. Ethan glanced to the gallery and laughed. It was about fine time to let Charly know he liked her too. He hurried down the drive in the rain then crossed the street and entered the very empty gallery to be.

Her strawberry-blonde friend and a guy who looked vaguely familiar but he couldn't place stood facing the door Ethan walked through.

Charly's back was to him. "It's hopeless, and no offense to you, Jason…"

The guy grinned and nodded in understanding. "None taken."

Charly sighed, with the weight of the world on her to the point her shoulders and curvy frame lifted then fell from the gesture. "But I'm swearing off men and kissing at this point."

*Not good.*

Her friend glanced from Ethan to Charly and shook her head no at the sexy gallery owner.

"Yes, Liz." Charly groaned in frustration. "No men, no kisses, and hell no to drama."

"You're just saying that," the strawberry-blonde told her, glancing again to Ethan then back at Charly.

"No, I am staying uninvolved. My ego can't handle it."

"Charly, you don't mean that," the guy told her and stepped toward her. He set his hands on her shoulders and turned her around to face Ethan.

She looked beautiful. Her big, brown eyes widened and a hand covered her mouth. "Oh, hell!" Her cheeks turned pink from embarrassment and she was the most perfect thing he'd ever laid eyes on.

Ethan laughed and stepped toward her. "Not quite, though my mother would argue it some days." He winked and grinned. "I'd settle for a hello."

She lowered her hand. "Hello?"

"Hello." Ethan then glanced to the guy, recognizing him. "You play for the Angels?"

"I do. I'm Jason, and you must be Ethan."

Confused, he nodded. "I am. How did you know that?"

"'Cause she never looked at me like that. We were just leaving." He slipped his arm around Charly's friend's waist and they stepped around her.

"Bye, Charly," her friend—Liz was it?—called out and laughed. "Have fun!"

Ethan turned as the couple slipped through the front entrance and the glass door closed behind them. He glanced back at Charly, who wore a very nervous and uncertain expression. His arms crossed in front of his chest and he studied the auburn beauty. "Now, what was this about swearing off men and kissing?"

## Chapter Six

Charly was so beautiful. Her shy innocence and good looks could steal any man's heart. She pulled her lower lip between her teeth and swallowed. Correction, she was beautiful and as sexy as hell. "What are you doing here?"

Ethan couldn't control the grin curling across his mouth. "I was talking to Cole."

She groaned and covered her face with her hands. "I forgot you knew each other."

"Kissing seems to be a big topic today. Actually, Cole and I have known each other for years and are good friends. Now, can I ask why you are swearing off men and kissing?"

She lowered her hands and frowned. "No, not without sounding like a tramp."

He didn't believe that for a minute. "I highly doubt that. Rumor is you're quite the lady."

"I try to be since I have a daughter to raise." She inhaled a deep breath. Her shoulders lifted then fell.. "I haven't had much luck with men and kissing lately. Cole told you about last night, huh?"

"Yeah."

"I can explain." Her voice was soft and faint.

He closed the distance between them. "Actually, let me explain something to you."

She blinked and remained quiet then her breath caught with the slightest hitch. The simple action shouldn't have been such a turn on, but ever since he had first laid eyes on her, standing in her kitchen on the phone with her smoke alarm blaring, he'd wanted her. He wanted her more now knowing that he affected her the same way she affected him. "I would say that you've kissed the wrong men and you should let me try."

"I wanted you to kiss me yesterday and I would've cancelled with Cole quicker than a heartbeat if you hadn't left." A breathy laugh escaped her and, again, her cheeks tinted pink. "Wow." She smiled as her nervousness prevailed. "That was blunt."

"Blunt is good, and I loved hearing that truth." He lifted his hand, he pushed a shoulder-length ringlet off her cheek, and tucked it back behind her ear. "I wanted to kiss you too, and I've regretted not doing so every other second of every other moment since." His hand slipped beneath the silky curls at the back of her neck. He lowered his head to hers and her long lashes closed. His other arm wrapped around her waist and pressed her full breasts against his chest. Her nipples were hard and seared his flesh through the fabric of their clothes. His lips touched hers and flames engulfed his body. Ethan's heart thudded in his chest and she gasped. Her mouth opened. After taking his time to slide his tongue over her full bottom lip, he slid inside the welcoming wet warmth.

Charly's tongue met his and entwined. A soft moan escaped against his tongue and his groin stiffened. His hand splayed across her lower back and slipped to her firm, denim-covered bottom. He held her against the ache in his pants and her arms snaked around his neck, pulling him closer. His hand dropped from her neck and joined his other hand, taking her other butt cheek in his hold. He wanted her in the worst way and his erection pulsed.

Deepening the kiss, images of her naked and groaning in pleasure beneath him as he worked in out of her wet walls decorated his mind. Would it be wrong to move her up against a wall and make love to her right there?

A slow hiss filled the room around them as it started to rain. Her lips pulled from his and his eyes opened. Charly's doe-like gaze met his and her puffy lips grinned. "That was the hottest kiss of my life." Her breath was ragged.

"Mine too." He glanced up to see the sprinklers spraying water down. "I think you need those checked. My guess, though, they sensed the heat." His gaze met hers again and she laughed. He chuckled and briefly touched her lips with his. "Let me see if I can figure out how to shut it down." Begrudgingly, he pulled his body from hers.

He paused and studied how she looked at that moment. Her white button-down shirt clung to her under the spray, revealing firm breasts tucked into a lace bra. She was soaked, but stunning. "And where is the power box?"

She laughed the most sensual, heartfelt laugh. "I think you found it, but since it's not me, you want to turn off — "

Ethan chuckled. "I like you turned on, but I need to turn the sprinklers off."

Heat darkened her eyes. Pure lust blinked at him and he became a man close to coming undone. Her weak and uncertain grin stroked his heart to beat faster. "Then try the office on your left."

Shaking his head, he headed to the office. He hurried in and noticed it was empty. Ethan noticed the metal box on the wall and shut everything down but his libido. Ethan was amazed he could walk with such a hard-on. The water stopped pouring from the sprinklers and everything was dark. He walked back out to the gallery. It had some light coming in from the windows, the type where you could see out, but from the sidewalk, no one could see in.

His eyes fell on Charly as he approached. She looked at him and smiled despite being soaked. "At least it's not raining on the inside anymore."

He glanced around at the water on the floor. "You have insurance, right?"

She nodded and smiled. "Yes. And apparently, I need a cleanup crew."

He grinned and understood. "As a fireman, I can recommend one." His gaze, with a mind of its own, raked over her wet body. Her clothes hugged every curve. He was jealous of her shirt and hungry for the strained nipples fighting the barriers of both the lace bra and cotton. "You should probably get home and change out of those clothes."

Charly groaned in frustration as if remembering something. "I would, but I can't go home and get out of my clothes."

The thought of her naked seared heat and nudged his libido, kicking his sex drive into gear. He swallowed hard and banished all erotic thoughts for the moment. "Is there a problem?"

She exhaled a slow, drawn out breath. "Jason drove me here with Liz. I have no way to get home without calling a cab, and I somehow don't think they are going to want my soaked butt parked on their seat. I need a ride."

"I'd be happy to ride you."

*Freudian slip. Dammit, I'm a gentleman, or have been raised to be one anyway.*

Her lips parted, her brows lifted, and surprise animated her features. "I mean, I can give you a ride." *I mean that literally.*

"I'd love for you to ride me." She flinched and cringed as an apologetic expression scrunched itself across her face. "I meant drive me. I would appreciate the ride."

Ethan chuckled again and couldn't believe she was just as overwhelmed by the chemical attraction as he was. The spark of heat had been there since he first laid eyes on her. "Let's get you home and out of those clothes." He closed his eyes and then opened them.

Charly's smile was sultry. "I was hoping you'd offer."

Ethan closed the distance between them. "Sweetheart, I'm more than offering." Her breath stopped as he lowered his head to hers. His lips touched her mouth in heated need. The thought of taking her home, getting her out of her clothes, and then driving into her made him wish they were already back at her place.

Charly's heart was still thudding as Ethan pulled his car into the driveway next to her truck. She turned and looked at him. "Can I offer you a towel and a hot cup of coffee?"

His grin flamed her skin and her body tingled. "Yeah, that would be great."

No man had any right to be this sexy. The way his wet denim shirt clung to him ignited heat through her body. "Unless you have to get back to the station."

He shook his head. "I actually started days off today. I went into the station for something to do."

"I could always give you something else to do." *Hell! I'm a blubbering maniac with sex on the brain. So this is what it feels like to be Liz and Jenna.*

Charly's lips parted, then she pulled her bottom lip between her teeth from her slight moment of hesitation. Maybe she would have her head on straight if he hadn't kissed her so—deliciously. "What I meant was, you can come in, or you don't have to come in. I'm easy either way."

Ethan's brows lifted and his smile turned wicked to the point of lustful.

She rethought that statement. "Well, not easy ever, but..." *To think I deal with naked men often. Why am I so nervous?* "I meant it's up to you." *Where is my brain?*

*In your wet thong,* the devil reminded.

*Try, try, try to be a lady,* the angel pleaded.

His long lashes blinked and his blue eyes held a twinkle of mischief. "I have time to come in. Let me get your door."

Ethan jumped out of the car and hurried around to her door before he opened it and continued to hold it as the rain poured down around. She slid out of the car and smiled at him then tilted her head and motioned to the door. She ran up the step with Ethan close behind and took shelter under the awning covering the front porch. Charly unlocked the bolt and handle then turned to the soaked fireman. "Come on in."

He glanced to the car. "Actually, let me grab my gym bag. I have clean, dry clothes in there."

She nodded and opened the front door then crossed over the threshold. Ethan ran over to the truck of his car, pulled out a small duffle bag, then hurried back toward the entrance. His body was defined by the wet clothes clinging to him and accented the strength of his shoulders, arms, and legs. Once he was out of the wet clothes, she was in no hurry to see him in dry ones—or any for that matter.

He stepped through the door and his chest grazed hers. Her nipples tightened and ached beneath the lace of her bra and the wet cotton shirt clinging to her. The cold was a contrast to the heat that radiated off his solid chest. His blue eyes turned navy as she shut the door and instinctively locked the bolt. "Let me get you a towel."

She stepped toward the hall and Ethan's hand wrapped gently around her wrist. Her skin heated from the slightest touch. Instinctively, she stopped and glanced at him. Her breath caught at the look of desire on his face and at how his Adam's apple rose and then slightly fell. "You should probably get out of your clothes."

"I was thinking the same about you." Considering how wet she was everywhere, her voice was incredibly dry.

Ethan glanced to her lips. She slid her tongue across them immediately, thinking that it would fix the new difficulty in swallowing. His gaze met hers and her breathing stopped. He took a single step and closed the distance between their bodies. "Maybe we should both get out of our wet clothes and warm up."

Charly's eyes widened and her nervousness returned. Was she really this out of practice? "Did you want coffee?"

"No, I think I'll start with you naked." His head lowered to hers and her eyes closed. His hand released her wrist and joined his other hand in a tight hold on her hips. Ethan's mouth came down on hers, warm and hungry. Her lips parted and her tongue sought his. She had to taste him, and the thought of being naked with him soaked her thong further. Thank the stars it was coming off in record time, at least she hoped.

Ethan's hands pressed her belly to his stomach and the hard bulge behind his zipper. She groaned and his hands slipped around her hips to her butt, pulling her in harder. Charly desperately wanted him inside her.

*Hell!*

"Stop!" She groaned against his tongue and lifted her lips. "You have a condom, right?"

His lips moved to her neck, planted a wet kiss at the nape, then lifted and his gaze met hers. "No."

Her body hummed. "Okay, go." His lips found her neck again and her fingers laced through his hair. She moaned as his tongue caressed the sensitive skin under her ear. "Oh, God! Stop."

Ethan pulled his lips from her neck again. "You don't have one either?"

"It's been a while." She swallowed hard and started doing the math. "Leigh's eight, divorced at two." Her breathing was ragged, as was his. "Six years."

"Six?" Hid brows lifted in disbelief.

She nodded and he backed her up against the wall. Her shoulders touched the hard surface, but the flesh of her bottom was still in his hands.

He cast a lopsided grin. "I thought I had it bad. Two years for me."

She nodded and wrapped her arms around his neck "Okay, go." His mouth came down hard on hers and she pulled her lips off his as his hands ground her harder against the rock hard length still tucked in his wet jeans. "Stop!"

His breath was even more ragged.

So was hers. "Are you healthy?"

"Yes, very." His voice was a rasp, and the seductiveness sent a shiver straight to her clit. "You?"

"Very."

A fleeting expression of uncertainty darted across his handsome face. "Is this a red light?"

She struggled for breath. "Green, I'm on the pill."

Ethan lips twitched into a breathless grin. "Perfect."

He let out a slow hiss and reclaimed her lips. His tongue thrust into her mouth and his hands lifted her gently. She wrapped her legs around his waist and tightened her hold around his neck. Her tongue entwined with his as he explored her mouth. She moaned softly against his tongue and her pussy ached. He smelled good, tasted great, and she wanted to feel his skin. His lips pulled off hers. "Stop!" he rasped.

Her lashes fluttered open and she couldn't control the smile. "Isn't that my line?" she asked between pants.

Ethan lifted a single brow and a grin teased his lips. His strong chest moved hard as he found air for his lungs. "Where's your daughter?"

"Next door making cookies with Jacque and no doubt tormenting Ambrose with kitty cat hugs and possibly doll clothes." She rested her head against the wall. "Can I take you up to the bedroom now?"

"No more stop lights?" he asked in a smooth, seductive whisper

Charly giggled and couldn't believe she was doing something so out of character and forward. "Depends, can you get naked on the move?"

"Hell yeah." He released his hold on her and safely set her down.

Removing her arms from around his neck, she tugged on his shirt and pulled it up over his head despite the fact it was a button-down. She tossed it to the floor and her gaze raked over him. The man was living art. Perfectly sculpted, his muscles rippled over his broad chest down to his defined six-pack. She slowly exhaled, pursing her lips together. He was gorgeous.

His fingers quickly undid the buttons on her top and pushed the wet cotton off her shoulders. It clung slightly from the wet, but fell off her shoulders, down her arms, and also hit the floor. A shiver ran over her. Charly grabbed his hand and led him to the bottom of the stairs. Reaching out, he enfolded her into his arms. His touch on her bare back flamed her skin as his fingers splayed and caressed the flesh. She slipped her hands to the buckle of his belt and quickly undid it. Her fingers captured the button of his jeans and tugged, then her fingers grasped the metal of the zipper and opened the teeth. Running her hand against his defined stomach muscles, she slid it lower into his boxer briefs and ran a slow finger against his rock hard length.

Ethan hissed again and his hands moved to the button fly of her jeans. "I am about thirty seconds from taking you on these stairs." His teeth gently nibbled on her lip as his hands worked her out of her jeans, taking the wet thong with them. The air of the room cooled her skin.

"Would it sound horrible if I said I don't care where you take me?"

"Did you lock the door?" His fingers caressed the skin of her leg and slowly slipped over the wet, shaved folds between her thighs. His finger teased gently.

"I always do," she told him as her knees weakened.

"Good girl," he whispered, and grazed his feathery touch over her clit

She wrapped her arms around his neck and brought her lips to his. He removed his fingers, cradled her back, and lowered her to the stairs. Ethan's tongue pried her mouth open and slid in as she felt the soft carpet on the stairs against her bottom. His lips lifted from hers and he quickly got out of the remainder of his clothes. Charly's lips formed an "oh." He certainly wasn't lacking in the *ladder* department. Ethan leaned into her and knelt on the stairs. He brought his hands around to her back and unclasped her bra. He gently peeled it off and tossed it over the banister railing.

"You are so beautiful," he whispered.

Her breath caught as his blue eyes blazed with desire. Never had a man looked at her so intently with the fire of lust blazing in his gaze. "I had similar thoughts about you."

His strong, handsome features softened and his lips curled into a smile. "As long as it's agreed." He lowered his head toward her and moved his hands to her breasts. His lips crushed against hers as his fingers found her taut nipples. Already stiff from the chill, his touch heightened her senses and they hardened further. She moaned against his tongue as he played and teased them beneath his touch. Her body ached in longing, and desire pooled between her legs. She laced her fingers through his hair and savored the feel of it softness in her hands.

His strong stomach pressed against her knees and she parted her legs for him. Sliding his hands from her breasts, he moved one hand to the small of her back and the other to the wet folds between her legs. His tongue explored her mouth as his finger gently stroked the surface. Ethan groaned and removed his fingers. He placed the other hand near the one at her lower back and grazed the tip of his erection where his fingers had left. The kiss deepened and his tongue delved further into her mouth as he entered her slowly. She locked her arms behind his neck and gasped slightly as his size filled her.

She lifted her lips from his and his eyes opened. Her body stiffened slightly. His dark lashes parted and his blue eyes rested on her. "Relax, no rush," his voice soothed in a seductive whisper. "You're incredible."

She let out a breath she didn't realize she had been holding and reclaimed his lips. He was the incredible one and his sensitivity only made her want him more. She gently slipped her tongue into his mouth and his hands tightened their hold on her. Her fingers played with the soft waves of his hair and, little by little, Ethan moved within her. He completely filled her and then some, but he felt good. She inched herself closer to him and scooted to the edge of the stair. He fell into a gentle rhythm and the pressure built across her. She couldn't get enough of him as he slowly picked up speed.

His tongue mated with hers and when he groaned, she knew he was holding back, but kept thrusting inside her. His lips rose from hers and found the tender flesh on her neck. His tongue teased it and his breath warmed her ear. She slipped her hands to his shoulders and pulled his strong, muscular chest flush against her straining nipples. The pressure continued to build and tighten across her. His lips kissed the lobe of her ear and, again, his breath danced across her skin.

The intimacy and intensity became her undoing. Her wet walls clamped around him and a whimper of pleasure parted from her as her orgasm broke free. A feral groan left Ethan and he thrust one more time. They climaxed together as he emptied his release inside of her.

Their bodies were damp with sweat and she could barely breathe. He struggled for air against her ear and slipped a hand to the back of her head. "Amazing and beautiful," he whispered in a raspy, breathless voice.

She hugged him close and her walls tightened and spasmed. "Maybe next time, we'll make it to the bedroom."

His chuckle was ragged. "Maybe, but I wouldn't count on it. The only thing I'd count on is that there will be a next time."

Charly sighed. She hoped so, because sex this hot with Ethan was going to become her favorite pastime. Suddenly, for the first time in weeks, she had the inspiration to paint.

Ethan grinned as he walked into the fire station. Yesterday had been an incredible afternoon and even a better evening. His knees were a little red still from the encounter with Charly on the stairs, but it had been a small price to pay. After they had quickly showered, he had stayed for dinner and Leigh had joined them with the cookies she had made with Jacque. She was animated and outgoing, and he had to admit that it had been a while since he had sat through a full-length animation on DVD. Technically, that while was a never, but it had been fun.

For once, being on days off wasn't so bad. He couldn't remember the last time he'd had plans that didn't involve his mother. He headed up the stairs to the office and quarters and his smile broadened.

"Oh, big shock! Look whose here on his day off," Bryce, one of the firemen, called. "Wow, Ethan, big enough smile?"

"No fear, guys, I'm not staying today. I have things to do," he explained, and sat down at the table in the kitchen.

"Your mom has more charity work that she is dragging you on?" Tony teased. He had worked with these guys for years and enjoyed their company. Not as much as Charly's, mind you.

"Actually, no, I'm going across the street to help the new gallery owner."

Eyebrows lifted.

"And is the gallery owner the shorter strawberry-blonde, or is it the leggy redhead?" Jim, another one of his men, asked as he sat at the table with a coffee.

"The strawberry-blonde is her friend. The leggy redhead," he told them.

"Damn, I knew it." Tony chuckled. "You should have seen this guy at the call." He lifted his brows to a couple of the others that had come in. "He was speechless."

"She's hot, and since it has been almost two years since Ethan has shown any interest in the female persuasion, I wish you the best of luck, man." Bryce raised his coffee mug and sipped from it. "Hey, do you know if she'll be able to get her hands on any of Joey Sinn's work?"

Ethan shrugged. He had to admit, he didn't know much about art outside of what his mother mentioned. He remembered his mom mentioning that artist. His brows furrowed. "I'm not sure. I can ask her for you."

"My sister saw this picture when she was in New York of a couple under a street lamp and was wondering if I could find a print for her. Thing is, no one can keep her stuff in stock."

This was news to Ethan, especially since he had no clue as to who Joey Sinn was. "Great artist, I take it?"

The guys laughed. "Man, that artist is the essence of sin and pleasure." Tony smiled and wiggled his brows. "My sister bought a greeting card for her friend's birthday and the guy was half naked, and let me tell you, he looked like he had just had the ultimate climax. His hand was resting on a woman's head and you can just imagine what she'd been doing to give him that look. Hell, I was almost jealous."

Ethan nodded. He sighed. It could get interesting, and not in a good way, if Charly did carry the artwork. "I'll find out for you. Joey Sinn is the artist's name?"

"Yeah, amazing artist. You just know that woman screams sexy. All her work is erotic and sinful. I bet she comes by her name honestly." Jim nodded and laughed. "I would love to give her inspiration."

Bryce snorted. "Maybe she's a big, fat chick that paints with a doughnut in her hand and a paintbrush in the other." Some of the guys debated that fact. "I mean, then of course there is every man's fantasy that she is a hot lady with a hotter body that needs to have sex constantly."

"This coming from a man who can't keep his fly done up." Tony laughed. "Bryce, your zipper comes undone as soon as you see a nice set of tits and a great ass. Remember the one call with the woman with the cat in the chimney? It was you that went back and cleaned her chimney, as I recall, and gave whole new meaning to rescuing the *pussy*."

Chuckling, Bryce nodded. "And she didn't complain. Unlike Ethan's mother did, while we're on the topic of sin."

Ethan's back stiffened. *Oh dear, now what?* "What about my mom?"

"Well, I went over to Mr. Wilson's art gallery, and one of the ladies was dropping off a print to be framed and it was like this three hundred thousand dollar picture that apparently was an heirloom. Very Rubenesque, my guess an original. Anyway, the women were naked and your mom went on about how that was the problem with society and the values. I mean, the picture was a print that was most likely a few hundred years old, and your mom went off about how society focuses on sex and blah, blah, blah."

Ethan groaned. "The woman needs a hobby. Trust me, the sooner I find her one, the better."

The men chuckled. "Hoping she will be side-tracked out of your sex life there, man?" Tony grinned.

"I doubt I could be that lucky." He stood and shook his head. "I wish I was, though. Anyway, guys, have fun at work and take care. I have to do something in the office and, unless you all miss me terribly, or things get out of control, I will see you all on Wednesday night."

He turned away and walked into the office. He quickly signed a couple reports, then escaped the office and station. His mind went over the conversation the guys had. He was suddenly very curious about Joey Sinn and hoped the guys were exaggerating. He also hoped that, if it was true, Charly carried very little of the artist's work. He waited for the walk light and frowned. After two years, the last thing he needed was for anything to heat up other than his relationship with Charly. The light changed and he smiled as he crossed the street. Now that the stoplights were out of the way, he wanted to see how far this relationship could go.

JT Schultz

## Chapter Seven

Oh yeah, it was a Monday. There was no disputing the fact as Charly couldn't even hear herself think as she stood in the gallery with the construction crew going on around her. It was just before lunch, she was starving, and as of the moment, still had no electrician. If she hadn't had such a terrific time the night before with Ethan and Leigh, her mood would even be worse. She glanced at her watch as the front door opened. Maybe it was Ethan. He had said he would stop and see her today. She hoped he did. Then again, he didn't really seem like the sort of guy that just said something without meaning it.

She turned to the door to see the alarm geek that had been at her house walk in. "Can I help you?"

"What, no knife this time?" he asked without greeting.

"One never knows what I have up my skirt, so let's not get smart, okay?" She smiled gently.

"I'd like to see what's up that skirt," one of the men in a hardhat told her.

Glancing at him, she smiled. "Not today. Besides, shouldn't you be working?"

"Darling, you have no idea what I can do with these hands," the man told her.

*For Christ's sake! Has every man taken a cheesy pick-up line class?*

She plastered a smile on her face and ran her palms down her denim skirt that was short, but far from revealing. "Then I suggest you get to work and show me. My gallery could use your hands. Not me, but thanks for the offer."

"I'd still like to take you out," the alarm geek assured with a flash of braces.

*Oh yeah, this a Monday all right.* "I don't think so. Why are you here?"

Alarm geek gave her a look as if she were a mental patient. "To put your alarm in." He gave her the once-over—a long, appreciative once-over. "I can put in whatever you need wherever you need it." He took in the floor that was still damp from the sprinklers the day before.

Thankfully, Ethan had called a company before dinner last night and had them come over there. She could only imagine that the leasing agent had been thrilled with hauling her ass down on a Sunday.

"I don't mind how wet it is," alarm geek added.

She groaned and silently swore she was going to barf. The come-ons just kept on, well, coming. *Just dump your coffee on the nerd*, the devil shouted. *Let him down easy; he's young and fragile*, the angel soothed.

He wiggled his brows and flashed his mouthful of metal. "I don't mind installing when it's wet."

"Actually, I have all of the lady's installation needs covered, so stick to alarms there, stud."

Charly glanced toward the door and her spirits lifted, bringing her lips into a smile. "Hi," she greeted Ethan.

"Hi." He glanced around and checked out the workers. The alarm dude rolled his eyes and set his toolbox down. Ethan looked back at Charly and smiled. "Part of your fan club?"

She grimaced and a sexy chuckle left him. "I hope not," she whispered.

"She never looked at any of us like that," the construction guy muttered, and turned back to the drywall.

Glancing over to the man, Ethan nodded and grinned. "Yeah, I get that a lot." He then rested his smile on Charly. "I'm happy to see you. I had a great time last night."

She swallowed and remembered the incident on the stairs. Her body trembled slightly and her panties dampened. "Me too." He had been so sweet to her daughter. "Leigh had fun too."

"She's cute like her mom." He winked and her breath caught. His gaze lowered to her lips, then met hers again. She saw lust illuminating in their blue depths. Her throat and mouth dried and swallowing was impossible.

The front door opened again and drew Charly's attention off Ethan. A guy in his late forties stood there in dusty clothes. "Can I help you?

"Yeah I have some furniture for Charly Jamieson?" He glanced around. "Wow, I see you're still under construction."

Charly smiled and stepped around Ethan. "Yes."

The guy dragged his gaze over her. It was a similar look to the one the alarm dude had given her. "I mean that toward the gallery, not you."

*I should have stayed in bed.* Her brows lifted. *In bed and with Ethan.*

She smiled at the man. "There are loading doors at the back. You can pull in there. I'll open them."

"I'd like you to open up so I can pull in." His tone was suggestive and his brows went up.

Hers descended and her lips turned into a frown. "Right." She turned and glanced to Ethan, who was studying the man.

Ethan's gaze found hers and he smiled. "Did you want me to go with you to the back?"

Her heart skipped a beat. "Would you mind?"

He stepped closer to her. "You look like you could go hit-on free."

"Unless of course you feel the need." Her voice was quiet and she smiled. "To hit on me, I mean."

He laughed and placed a hand at her lower back as they headed to the warehouse area of the gallery. "I'd love to do a hell of a lot more than that."

Her breathing was shallow, next to nonexistent. "I can live with those terms." A loud rattle echoed to the front from the back loading doors and she sighed. "I think he wants in my bay."

Ethan tilted his head and placed a hand at the small of her back as they walked toward the sound. "I think he does too, but he is only putting furniture in the gallery."

Laughing, she was glad that she hadn't imagined the delivery guy's interest. She led Ethan through a large white door to a garage that she was going to be using as mostly a warehouse. She sipped at her coffee as Ethan walked to the back and opened the large metal sliding door.

The truck backed in and Charly glimpsed around. She wondered silently if she was going to be open on time. Sighing, she knew that she would. Having any work of the remarkable Joey Sinn was another question. With the way her work as Joey Sinn kept going up in price, she was amazed that the people still wanted it. The one painting she had limited prints done up of had sold very well. She had tested the waters out in California not far from here and in New York.

The galleries had sold out and begged her for more. She had sent the additional prints from New York the day she left. Everyone wanted Joey Sinn. Lately, everything with a dick wanted Charly Josephine Jamieson as well.

She turned and glanced to Ethan, who was studying her. There was only one man she really wanted, despite the rainfall of offers and the downpour of men. He cast a wicked grin as the men started removing large shelves off the truck. She removed her eyes off Ethan to the large, metal shelf that had paint supplies on it. If they weren't careful, they were going to knock it over. "I think you need to move that a little more to the left."

"Trust us, ma'am, we know what we're doing," the older guy that had raked his eyes over her earlier like she was a race car replied.

She glanced again to the metal shelf. "I really think—"

Cut off by the sound of the heavy wood the men were carrying coming hard against the metal shelf the supplies resided on, she glanced up as it pivoted then swerved. She lifted her shoulders and braced herself as the shelf teetered. Her eyes widened as it started to tip over and directly toward her.

"Charly!" Ethan's sexy voice reached her the same time he did.

His strong hands grabbed her upper arms. The coffee in her mug splashed up over the little hole in the lid to her hand. She dropped the paper cup as her body lifted and moved, then stopped, pressed hard against Ethan's solid chest. His one arm was wrapped tightly around her waist now and a hand cupped the back of her head. Her face was shielded against his strong shoulder. The shelving unit came down and the cans of paint popped their lids. It was an explosion of color and, in less than sixty seconds, it was over. She and Ethan stood, coated like rainbows from the airborne paint.

Lifting her head from his shoulder, she glanced at him. Okay, not completely covered, but they were definitely colorful. She reached up and brushed Ethan's cheek. Trying to remove what looked like a teal color from his skin, she ended up smudging it. His eyes were intent on her face, most likely the only part of her paint free. She felt thick liquid drip and run down her bare legs. It was the look on Ethan's face, completely intense and sexier than hell, that left her heart racing and her breath stuck in her throat. "Thank you, you saved me."

His hand caressed her hair and he pulled it away to reveal red and yellow. "I'm not sure if us standing here resembling a bag of jelly beans is a full-fledged rescue."

She smiled. "I actually love jelly beans."

Chuckling, Ethan wrapped his other arm around her. "Me too." His gaze took in her paint-covered hair and shoulder, and then met hers. "You actually look really good in these colors."

She nodded and, as his face drew near hers, she closed her eyes. His breath teased her skin. "You know, maybe we should have moved it a little more left," the delivery driver told them.

Denied the kiss, she opened her eyes. Ethan glanced around her. "What was his first clue?" he whispered.

Charly laughed and turned in his arms.

"What the hell happened in here?" Cole demanded as he entered the room, shook his head at the delivery driver, then glanced over to Ethan and Charly. He stepped around the paint splatters on the floor and walked over to them. Ethan's hold on her didn't move. Cole looked to his arms around her waist and smiled. "I'm glad you took my advice," he told Ethan. He turned to Charly. "I guess you definitely won't be taking me up on my proposal, huh?"

She giggled. "Sorry, Cole, but the answer is still no."

"You proposed?" Ethan asked. The amusement in his tone wasn't hard to miss.

"I thought it might work, but it's worked out better, I think." He then frowned at the mess around them. He narrowed his gaze. "You guys need to go get cleaned up. I recommend going over to the fire station and hosing off there."

"I can grab a shower there, I guess." Ethan groaned. "But I used my change of clothes yesterday after the sprinklers went off here."

"I was wondering about the traces of water. What set them off?"

Charly's cheeks flamed and she was dead certain they were redder than the paint in her hair. "Uh…"

"I kissed her," Ethan told him in the same tone he would as if discussing a basketball game.

She turned to Ethan. "Actually, you have your clothes from yesterday at my house. I washed them this morning."

Cole laughed. "Must've been a hell of kiss. Listen, Charly, Ethan, go get cleaned up and I'll keep an eye on things here." He looked to the bay door that was open and turned back. "Is there a lock on the inside of that thing?"

"No, and the one on it now can easily be broken," Ethan answered dryly.

Bouncing her attention between the two men, she sighed. "You think I need something stronger?"

"I don't know. You get cleaned up and I'll go through here with the alarm guy and see what I think. I may recommend a lock specialist."

"Sure, let me know what they say and I'll cut them a check." She turned to Ethan. "We can take my truck; it has seen a lot of paint. I would hate for your car to get dirty." She reached into her pocket and pulled out the keys.

"Can I drive?" He lifted his brows.

*Absolutely, you can drive me all afternoon if you feel the need.*

"Of course." She handed him the ring in her hand and, for some strange reason, felt like it was for more than the truck she had passed the keys to.

Ethan couldn't believe that she had passed over the keys. Most women had issues with men driving. Charly had none. It wasn't that he was a chauvinist. He just needed something to concentrate on other than her legs. Her now paint covered legs. There was no way he would have enough control not to touch her while she was driving. She was too beautiful and heated more than his blood. She impassioned his entire soul. He unlocked the handle for her and they stepped into the house. Ethan shut the door and locked the bolt. He was glad that Cole was willing to help her out by staying at the gallery and making sure the security was tight.

"What's wrong?"

He glanced at the woman that had already brought so much to his life and whose smile he couldn't resist. "Cole asked me the other day to keep an eye on the gallery, and now he was there today to check your security. Are you in trouble?"

*Be honest with her.*

He debated amount then proceeded. "He mentioned that you had a problem in New York."

She nodded and her expression drew hesitant. "That's why I moved here. The stalker at one point even got into my place in New York. Let's just say, I didn't feel safe anymore."

Sighing, Ethan stepped toward her. "Sweetheart, if you ever need anything, you let me know. Cole is a friend and, despite the differences in the past, I know he's concerned."

Her eyes lost their sparkle, but she nodded. "I know."

Wrapping his arms around her, he grinned. "I was going to kiss you at the gallery."

"The last time you kissed me here we didn't even make it up the stairs." Her voice was soft and her slender throat moved slightly from a hard swallow.

"This is true," he admitted, and lowered his head. Her long lashes fluttered closed and his lips claimed hers. Heat surged through his body and he parted his lips, slowly allowing his tongue to taste her. Her lips opened for him and he slid his tongue into her mouth.

Her hands caressed his shoulders and he pressed her closer to him as he deepened the kiss. A soft moan left her and his groin stiffened. He lifted his lips from hers and her eyes opened. "Why don't we get up the stairs while we can?"

She inhaled nervously. "Will you join me in the shower?"

"I had every intention of it," he confessed as his erection grew harder and his desire flamed.

"Smart man."

His gaze dropped to her puffy lips, evidence that he had kissed her. She stepped out of his arms and walked to the stairs. Charly tossed a look over her shoulder and tilted her head to encourage him to come. If she looked any sultrier he was sure he would have climaxed there. The woman had no a clue how much sexual electricity she sent through his body. "I would move really fast, sweetheart, or its going to be sex on the stairs again."

She flipped her hair back and took off around the corner with a giggle. There was no way now that Ethan wasn't going to take off after her. Running into a bedroom, she laughed again. He crossed the threshold and stopped. It looked like something out of a Roman Palace. Elegance in rich burgundies and gold met him. The white sheers draped over the head board and created romance all around.

He glanced to the walls and noticed the pictures. They had a Roman theme and looked classic. He turned to Charly in surprise and awe. "This is a really nice room."

She cringed. "That never has seen any action. Everything is new pretty much except the artwork."

"I can think of a few things to do on that bed."

She laughed and crooked her finger at him. "Come, we'll start with a shower."

"Oh yeah." He walked into the bathroom and it, too, was done with a Roman theme. The tile and everything around it was expensive and rich. He glanced at the tub, designed for two, and the shower that not only had a bench in it, but had multiple showerheads. He let out a low whistle. "I knew the houses in this area were expensive, but wow."

Charly leaned into the shower and turned it on. The spray started and she looked at him. "I never really thought about it."

"Why do I have this feeling you're not the average single mom?" This was a far cry from the warm home he had grown up in. His house growing up had been small and he'd watched his mom struggle. The day he'd paid off her house and then the day he'd bought her a new car was his way of thanking her for her all she had done.

Pulling her lip between her teeth, she blinked at him. "I've worked really hard. I don't date much and I guess I wanted a life better than the lower middle class one I grew up in. I went to school with a lot of rich kids and I wanted to be like them. I was always a little different, being heavily into art."

Ethan took in the room and smiled at her. "You've done well for yourself."

"It came at a price, thus the stalker."

He hated that look of sadness on her face and moved toward her. He cupped her face in his hands. "Why me?" His voice was soft and he wasn't even really sure why he was asking.

"There was just something about you from the moment I saw you. I think you had the same effect on me that I had on you." She debated a moment then sighed and met his gaze. "You were perfect."

"And I don't think you could possibly be any sweeter."

Her dark eyes sparkled. "I could be if you would get naked and join me in the shower."

Laughing, Ethan released her face and stepped back. "I think I adore that bluntness the most." She peeled off her once black t-shirt and revealed a lace, black bra. "Okay, I adore that bra too."

He couldn't remember when getting naked with a woman had been not only arousing, but playful. This was different. Charly was different. "You should see the thong that goes with it." She dropped her denim skirt to the floor.

Ethan groaned. She had an incredible body. It was far from fat, but curvy in all the right spots. He removed his clothes as she slipped the black lace underwear off and stood naked in front of him. Her attention fell to his hard erection as it sprang free; her gaze rose again. Desire blazed in her dark eyes and she opened the shower door. She stepped in under the spray. "I hope you don't mind it hot."

Ethan kept the comment about it already being hot to himself and stepped in the shower with her. "I can handle a lot of heat."

"As a fireman, I bet you can."

Flames had nothing on Charly Jamieson. He reached out and gently brought her against him. His skin heated further. "The water is perfect," he whispered as colorful paint ran from her hair in a watery stream over her shoulder to the drain below. "I love the way you look with wet hair."

Her breathing was shallow and she pressed her pelvis against his already aching hard-on. "I believe you. Seems it always ends up wet around you." Her laugh was light and breathy. "Then again, so does my thong."

"Perfect." He lowered his mouth to hers and allowed his hands to slide over her wet body. Her eyes closed and his lips came down on hers. He was pleased to discover her mouth already parted and her tongue seeking his. His tongue entwined with hers and desire coursed through his veins.

Her hands ran over his body and her nipples hardened against his chest. He moaned and lifted his lips from hers. Their bodies completely soaked from the water of the spray, he slid his hands over her. She stepped out of his arms and smiled wickedly. She slipped her hand in his and led him to the bench. "I couldn't help noticing your knees were red from yesterday."

Her voice hit every nerve in his body with a caress. Ethan struggled for breath and for his voice. "What did you have in mind?"

She laughed evilly and reached for his other hand. "Have a seat and I'll show you."

*Where the hell has she been my whole life?*

He sat on the bench and noticed the room was filling with steam. She dropped to her knees and looked up at him through her lashes. *Holy hell!* Her hand wrapped around his length and her head lowered. Slowly, her tongue grazed the side and then teased the head of it as her hand stroked in a gentle rhythm. Her mouth lowered and she took him in. He groaned loudly and cupped the back of her head in his hands. Ethan fought for his control. He laced his fingers through her tresses and moaned again. Gently, he lifted her head and she blinked up at him.

Carefully, he slid his hands under her arms and helped her up. She swayed her hips and brought one knee up to rest against his hip, then lifted the other against his other hip. His arms went around and held her. Her arms braced against the glass wall of the shower and gradually slid down and around his neck as her head dropped toward his. Her mouth lowered to his as the tip of his length teased her entrance. She moaned in pleasure as she slid over him, her tight, wet walls engulfing him. His tongue glided over her lower lip and he didn't move until her body had adjusted to him. He didn't want to hurt her and knew she was not used to this. That alone made her more special. Her lips and tongue taunted his and her body moved up, then down, and Ethan tightened his hold on her.

He loved the way her walls twitched as her orgasm built. He held back, though he had to admit, he wasn't sure how long that would last. She was like no other woman he'd been with or had ever known. Charly's pace picked up and he moved his hips slightly, afraid if he moved too much she would slip. Her hands slid to his shoulders and her grip tightened. She removed her lips from his and a soft gasp of a wail left her. Her walls squeezed around him and her body shuddered in climax. Ethan groaned as he found an intense release. Charly's body gave another slight tremble and she brought her head back and looked at him as she climaxed again. Her breath was ragged and he was sure that, if he didn't take air into his lungs soon, he was going to black out.

Charly's hands slipped to the back of his neck and she brought her chest against his. His hands gently stroked her back. A strange sound filtered through his satiated mind. Her body snapped back and her mouth dropped open. "Oh no!"

"Hell!" he cursed with a chuckle as she scrambled off him. He threw open the shower door. He knew what the sound was. He grabbed a thick, huge, fluffy towel and wrapped it around his waist. "I didn't even hear it go off."

She cringed as she turned off the water and stepped out. "Me either, but I was more intent on getting you off. I forgot that, if the bathroom door isn't closed, the steam will trigger the smoke detector in the bedroom."

Laughing, he hurried to the bedroom door and came to a halt. His eyes widened in horror. "Sweetheart, make sure you're covered."

"What, honey?" she asked, and then halted. "Damn!"

He snuck a glance to see that she was in a thick, black terry robe and more than covered. He looked back to the hall. His men started to laugh, whistle, and clap.

"Nice one, Ethan," Bryce chuckled. "How could you not hear the alarm going off? And there was so much talk about me keeping my pants on," he teased and whistled long.

Ethan couldn't believe he was standing in only a towel. This was the most embarrassing thing he could have experienced. Nope, his men actually going in the bathroom would have topped that. There was movement at his side and Charly stepped closer to him. He inhaled deeply. "Charly, these are the guys I work with."

He glanced at her to see her cheeks stained pink. It was most likely a combination of the hot sex and the fact that they now had an audience. She nodded slowly and took his team in.

"Looks like I'm not the only one that helps the ladies out," Bryce told him with another chuckle.

"But you don't get red knees in the process," Jim pointed out with a wave of his fingers to Ethan's legs.

Gasping, Charly placed her hand gently on Ethan's arm. "And here, honey, I thought your men were trained for any situation."

Ethan closed his eyes and laughed, then opened them to shoot a look to Jim. The man was stunned. Tony and Bryce slapped his shoulders and snickered. "Burnt by the babe," Jim sneered, and then laughed.

"Charly, I think you're exactly what our man Ethan here needs," Bryce told her.

"Well, that's great," she purred, and from the corner of his eye, he caught the smile on her lips. "Since there is no fire, and I do appreciate your concern for my safety, let me thank you for not stepping further than the bedroom door."

"I was so hoping the call was over more of that chicken," Bryce told her.

"Not this time, but if you'd be good flame fighters and go back out to your truck, maybe I can swing by the station with some this week."

Bryce lifted his brows. "You're kicking us out?"

Tony laughed. "So that chicken is definitely part of the deal?"

Sighing, Charly laughed. "Yes, boys." She glanced at the long tube in the hall that flowed down the stairs. "I think I've had enough hose for the moment."

His men's eyes widened and Ethan slapped a hand to his mouth. She was definitely a lot of spark and had just officially set his heart on fire. There was no denying the fact. He was falling in love with her.

## Chapter Eight

"I am so grateful your colleagues didn't come into the bedroom, or heaven forbid, the bathroom," Charly told Ethan as she turned from the counter and passed him a coffee. They were both dressed in clean, paint free clothes and waiting for Leigh to get home from school.

"I have to admit, I'm equally as glad, especially considering what a great shower that was."

She smiled and set her mug down on the counter. She stepped toward him and wrapped her arms around his neck. He circled her waist with the arm that wasn't holding the coffee. "I'm really glad I met you." Her eyes scanned his face. He was so handsome and happy.

"You're an amazing lady."

She stretched up slightly and grazed her lips against his. Gently, he nibbled on her lips and tightened his hold around her waist. The handle of the door tried and she jumped back. There was thudding knock. "Ah, Leigh must be home."

Nodding, she headed over to the door and unlocked it. Pulling it open, Leigh walked in with one of her little friends and grinned. "Mom, this is Nicole. Nicole, this is my mom. She is opening a gallery and paints pictures."

"Hi, Nicole," she greeted, and shut the door. Charly nodded at the little girl with big, blue eyes and curly blonde hair.

Leigh turned and squealed. "Ethan!" She moved over to him and wrapped her arms around his waist. She stepped back and looked up at him. "You missed me, didn't you?"

Chuckling, Ethan smiled at her daughter. "I did."

Leigh glanced over to Nicole and smiled. "This is Ethan; he's a friend of my mom's."

Stepping around the girls, Charly walked over to her mug and reached for it.

"Is he the kind of friend that spends the night?" the little girl asked.

Coughing and sputtering liquid, Ethan slammed his mug down on the counter and covered his mouth. Charly set her mug down and stepped to his side. "Are you okay?"

"No," Leigh answered. "He hasn't spent the night yet."

"Fine," Ethan told her, and headed over to the sink to wash his hands. Charly looked back at the girls.

Nicole looked like she was digesting this information. "My mom has two guy friends that spend the night. Never at the same time, though. That would be awkward." She turned to Charly. "So, are you divorced and going through a self-discovery phase as well?"

Ethan shot Charly a skeptical glance. She shrugged and focused again on the little girl. "No, actually, I have been single for most of Leigh's life. I think I discovered myself when she was two."

"Oh, so you're past your sexual revolution?"

*Oh my God! This isn't an eight-year-old, it's a reincarnated women's libber.*

"Honey, do you and Leigh want some cookies and milk?"

*What the hell do I say? Chances are she can't spell sexual, or revolution.*

"Cookies and milk will be good, and then we can talk, right, Leigh?"

Sighing with relief, Charly stepped over to the fridge and pulled open the door.

As Charly reached in for the milk, Nicole cleared her throat. "Over our snack, I can tell you what to expect once he does start spending the night."

Leigh glanced at Ethan and tilted her head as she studied him. "Ethan, are going to be spending the night?"

"Wow, uh..." His brows furrowed. "Well, I think your mom and I discussed staying for supper again, but—you know what? I'll grab you the cookies. Where are they?" He turned to Charly, blinked, and shook his head. The doorbell went as she stepped next to Ethan at the counter.

"What is that mother teaching her child?" she whispered.

"No clue," Ethan responded equally as quiet as the doorbell went again and Leigh walked over to the door.

She opened it and Charly's heart sank. *That's so dangerous!*

"Hello, sweetie, is your mom home?" a strange male voice asked.

"Leigh, get away from the door," she snapped at her daughter, a little colder and harsher than she maybe should have. Leigh shot her a wide-eyed expression and scurried over to Nicole.

Ethan glanced at the two girls and walked over to the door. "Can I help you?"

"Yes, I'm Henry, her mailman, and I just wanted to hand her mail to her personally. I couldn't get it all in her mailbox. You must be the husband."

"Actually, I'm—"

"Here you go." The mailman laughed. "Have a great day."

Waiting in the kitchen, Charly poured a glass of milk for the girls. The front door shut and she passed the glasses to them. She turned to Ethan, whose hands were full of mail. Her heart lurched into her throat. Staring at the thick stack of envelopes in Ethan's, she became sick to her stomach. Slowly, she turned to the cabinet and pulled out the container that had the cookies Leigh and Jacque had baked the day before. Her hands started to shake. She had to stay calm. Charly shut the cupboard door and turned to her daughter. Thrusting the container of cookies at Leigh, she struggled to find her voice. "Leigh, why don't you and Nicole go play up in your room?"

Her little girl took the cookies and stared wide-eyed at the mail in Ethan's hand. "Let's go, Nicole." The two girls moved toward the entrance of the kitchen and Leigh glanced back. "Just throw the black ones out." Her young voice was bland and void of all emotion. "We're still safe, right Mom?"

"Yes, dear," she answered. The girls walked around the corner and their footsteps echoed on the stairs.

Charly exhaled a slow breath and turned to Ethan, who glanced at the envelopes in his hand, then rested his eyes on her. "You're as white as a ghost." He set the mail on the counter and started separating the black ones into a pile. "There are twenty-five black envelopes. Why would Leigh want you just to throw them out?"

She was stronger than this. "Do any of them have a return address?"

Frowning, Ethan started to skim through them. "No. None of them, and they all have the same writing and ink. A silver, metallic-looking..." His words died and he spun around, realization etched across his face.

"I never put in a forwarding address."

"These aren't forwarded from your old address, Charly. These are all addressed to this address."

"Twenty-five, that's exactly how many days I've been out of New York." To her own ears, her voice was strained, weak, and lost.

Slowly, he lifted his cell phone from his hip and punched a number. "Yeah, Cole, I think you had better come over to the house. We have a slight problem." He paused. "Perfect, have them lock up and get over here." He hung up the phone. "Your friends Liz and Jenna just showed up at the gallery. Cole is going to have them lock up and he's on his way."

Worry etched itself across his handsome features and he stepped closer to her. "I'm scared, Ethan." Her voice was a mere whisper. Her heart pounded hard and heavy as her brain digested the fact her stalker knew where she was.

He nodded and pulled her into his arms. She buried her face in his shoulder and wrapped her arms around him. "Don't be scared, Charly. It will all be okay."

She stepped out of his arms. Hot tears stung her eyes and coated her lashes. "No, Ethan, it's not going to be okay. I have no idea as to who this fan is. I left a life and a successful business and I came across the country to start over.

The fan won't let me be and it's really hard to strike back at the unknown."

His brows furrowed slightly. "Fan? You mean the stalker is a fan of your former gallery?"

*Not good, I almost revealed everything. I want to trust him, but I really don't know him.*

She debated a moment. The angel snorted, *you may not know him, but it didn't stop you from having sex with him – more than once.* The devil on her other shoulder groaned. *Shut up, she needed sex and he's a decent guy. He looks worried.*

"They believe so, the police in New York."

Ethan's gaze darted around the kitchen, then fell back on her. "So you really meant that success had its price."

"Yeah, that was a literal moment and not a metaphoric one."

Blinking, his lips turned into a small smile. "Are you always quick with comebacks?"

"When I'm not terrified, I'm worse."

His features softened. "I know this is going to sound really crazy, but I really like you and I know I'm falling for you. I won't let anyone hurt you. I know a lot of people." He pointed to the stack of black envelopes, but his eyes never left her. "That is out of control."

"That is minor. That tells me that, whoever it is, is back to one a day."

"How many were you getting a day?" His deep baritone was more than terse.

"Two, sometimes three." Charly pulled her bottom lip between her teeth and experienced

165

a whirlwind of emotions. She really liked Ethan. Hell, she adored him, and for a fleeting second, imagined that they could have an amazing relationship. Now she wasn't so sure. Stacks of envelopes from a crazed fan would deter any normal guy.

"What are you thinking?"

*You don't want to know.*

"I may not be the right woman for you." There, she said it. The words were out in the open and her heart ached a bit.

His brows lifted and his smile broadened. "Sweetheart, if you think that some psycho is going to stop me from spending time with you, then you're completely wrong." He took her hand and stepped closer to her. His strong arm wrapped around her waist, and for a fleeting moment, she had a small assurance she was safe. "Maybe I need to spend more time with you."

Exhaling the breath that she didn't realize she'd been holding, she nodded, then smiled faintly. She really liked Ethan and was falling in love with him, if it was possible to do so soon. "You know, that may not be such a bad idea."

"I knew you would see things my way." He grinned, then lowered his lips to hers. Her body relaxed at the touch of his lips and his breath on her skin. Maybe things weren't so bad.

Ethan was far from amused. In fact, he was downright pissed off. Scowling, he rested his attention on the contents of the dining room table. He glanced over to Charly, who leaned against her large patio doors and stared out at the night sky. She looked a million miles away. He glanced to her friends Jenna and Liz talking quietly on the sofa. Jason walked in from the kitchen and over to Charly. He pressed a glass of red wine into her hand. She took the goblet from him and only nodded in gratitude. Jason then stepped over to the sofa and took a seat next to Liz on the sofa. With his mind spinning out of control, Ethan's gaze fell on Cole, who sat at the table with him going through the cards.

"This person is really messed in the head," Cole told him, lifting his gaze and meeting Ethan's.

Ethan held up one of the offending cards. "I love how the words on this have been scratched out in black marker and changed to more sadistic ones." He tossed it down and shook his head. He glanced over to Charly. Her eyes fixed on him. She shook her head and turned back to the window.

She was scared and unnerved. Whatever security she thought she had created for herself and Leigh had been ripped away from her by the arrival of the black envelopes.

Charly had ordered pizza for Leigh and her friend Nicole and told them they could eat and watch movies in the bedroom. She didn't want her daughter exposed to this anymore than she had to be. Ethan admired her for that. Charly had opened every one and looked at them, believing not to do so would be cowardly. She had brass, that was for sure. Ethan pulled himself out of the chair and walked over to where she stood. Sighing, she shifted her weight and her gaze fell back on him. "I'm sorry, Ethan."

He wanted to touch her. He wanted to wrap her in his arms, but wasn't sure how she would react to that with an audience. "There's no reason to be sorry."

She blanched and hesitation darkened her pretty features. Something was running through her head. He was clueless, though, as to what. "I—"

"What I don't get is this whole bit about 'I know who you are.'" Cole's voice cut off whatever she was going to say.

She glanced to Liz and Jenna and their eyes widened. She met Cole's studious expression.

Blinking at her, Cole held up one of the sadistic Valentines. "Any ideas?"

Casting a sideways glance to Liz and Jenna again, Jenna shook her head no. Charly turned again to Cole. "No, not really."

His friend glanced to Jenna. A curious look crossed his face and he turned to Ethan. What could he say? He knew the women knew something and weren't saying anything. By the expression on Cole's face, he knew it too.

Cole stood and glanced around the room of Charly's upscale living and dining room. He walked over to where an easel stood with a cloth draped over it and touched the cloth. He glanced to the walls and eyed the artwork.

Ethan was curious as to what Cole was thinking. Finally, his friend turned to Charly and smiled. "Can I look under the cloth at the picture on the easel?"

"Uh—it's just something I'm working on." She pulled her teeth between her lips, revealing she was nervous, very nervous. Charly darted a quick glance to Liz and Jenna again, and it wasn't hard to notice they were just as nervous. She focused her attention back on Cole. "Actually, I would rather you see it when it's done."

Cole nodded and stepped closer to where Ethan stood with Charly. "What aren't you telling me?" His face softened. "Charly, I can't do my job if I don't know everything."

Charly sipped her wine and her face lost color. Grief filled her eyes. "I have sold a few paintings and I think it's because of that. Only I paint under an alias."

Chuckling, Cole nodded. "See, that was pretty painless."

"For you," she answered. "You just had to stand there and look cute."

Cole's brows shot up. "Do you always just speak before thinking?"

"Traditionally, it has worked for me so far."

Cole cast a grin to Ethan. "She's perfect for you. I mean that, buddy." He started to laugh. "You have your hands full with her." He glanced back to Charly. "I will take the envelopes and notes with me and make sure that the gate guard tightens up on who comes in this area."

"Thanks, Cole," she mumbled.

"I am also going to want you to tighten the security up at the gallery. I had a locksmith go through it and he has suggested a complete change. Especially at the back bay door."

Sighing, Charly sipped again on her wine and nodded. "Arrange something for tomorrow and I'll make sure my checkbook is handy."

Cole nodded, then walked over to the table and picked up the love notes and threatening letters with their black envelopes. He turned back to Charly. "I'll see you tomorrow at the gallery. If you decide you have more to tell me, call me, or get Ethan to give me a shout."

She only nodded. Cole glanced to her friends on the sofa. "It was good seeing you all. Hopefully, next time it will be under better circumstances." His eyes lingered on Jenna a minute, then he turned to Ethan.

"I'll walk you out." Ethan led Cole out of the living room toward the front door then turned to his friend "Just how serious is this?"

Cole glanced into the living room then met his gaze. "Let's just say that whoever sent these is obsessed with her. My guess, it's some guy. I'm curious about her artwork, though. I mean, look at this place, Ethan. She's doing more than a little well for herself."

"She hasn't done anything wrong."

"No, but whatever she's done, she's done well, and someone wants to be part of it. See what you can find out about the artwork she's sold. Maybe there's a clue there. She's hiding something and that could cost her and her daughter a lot more than the painting hanging above the fireplace."

"I don't know much about art; is it expensive?"

Cole chuckled. "My guess is about fifty thousand. I wonder if she knows Joey Sinn? Now there is an artist. Sex and sin...let's just say — artist has talent."

Ethan frowned. "I can ask her. Everyone seems taken with Joey Sinn."

"Not everyone. Your mother would hate her."

There was a shock. His mother hated everything that had a warm exterior. As much as he loved his mother and would do anything for her, he wondered if she even disliked small, furry animals. It wasn't that his mother was cold. She just looked at love and life in a certain way. A completely different way than Ethan did. Now he kept from having a life so he wouldn't have to argue with her. "Well, thanks, Cole, and I'll let you know if she opens up. I think she's pretty guarded."

Cole nodded and opened the door. Ethan shut it and thought for a moment. Who was Joey Sinn? What was it that made the world marvel? He was going to have to find out.

Charly shut the door and sighed. She had gotten Nicole off with her mother, Leigh bathed and in bed. Then, after chatting about art, gossip tabloids, and Jason's last A's game that Ethan was completely into, she leaned against the door, drained. Not physically, but the silence was golden.

"You okay?" Ethan asked softly as he stood in the entrance of the living room by the stairs.

"It's been a long day."

"You aren't dwelling on the stalker, are you?"

"No." She shook her head and stepped toward him. His arms reached out and placed his hands on her hips. Tugging gently, he pulled her to him. "I try not to. I would go crazy if I did. Most days I try and convince myself that life is normal."

Sighing, Ethan circled his arms around her waist. "It's getting late."

"Yeah," she agreed. She didn't want him to go. As much as she loved her friends, she was happy to see them leave. Ethan, on the other hand, was different. "I suppose you need to get going."

A strange emotion flickered in his gaze and he let go of her. He turned slightly and glanced around the living room. His eyes fell on the canvas covered by the cloth and he looked back at her. "I admit I'm curious about what's under the cloth."

"Did you want to see?"

He studied her with a broad grin and nodded. He was a hunky, delicious man, but for those fleeting seconds, he resembled a little boy.

"Come on over," she told him, and walked over to the easel. She had no clue why she was doing this. Right, because her mind, in thirty seconds flat, lost all control from Ethan's smile. Her desire and attraction overruled logic.

"You wouldn't let Cole or anyone else see it."

She flashed him a grin. "No, I didn't want them to see. I guess because, as insane as this sounds, it's a little personal and I had a bit of painter's block after I moved. Then I woke up one morning and had this perfectly clear image in my head of what to paint. So I started. Only, with the gallery opening in just over a couple weeks, and the craziness of my daughter and my friends, who insist on having to stop by, I haven't really gotten back to it."

Carefully, his strong hands touched the soft material and for a fleeting second, Charly was jealous of the sheet. He lifted the cover up and stared at the eyes, almost the only thing on the canvas. The eyes of amazing blue that obviously were—

"You painted this?" He sounded stunned.

"Yes."

He turned and blinked at her. "You started to paint me from memory?"

Smiling weakly, she shrugged. "Let's just say you had my attention from the moment you walked into my house."

He glanced back at the painting and shook his head. "You're very good." With care, he covered the painting again and stared at her. "I'm really impressed and completely flattered." His gaze locked with hers and her breath caught. Desire blazed in his blue depths. "It's getting late and I know that you have to be at the gallery tomorrow."

There it was again, the longing. The wishing that he would stay. "I guess that means you should probably go."

Nodding, he closed the distance between them. "I should, but..." His voice trailed and he cast a sideways glance at the cloth over the easel. "Without sounding forward, I want to stay." His voice was a husky whisper that caressed her skin.

"I want you stay; I wasn't sure how to ask without sounding — "

Ethan's lips claimed hers and cut off her words. His hands grasped her hips and he drew her closer to him. He pressed her body against the rise in his jeans and her body flamed. Her lips parted and his tongue thrust in. Her arms wrapped around his neck and her breasts strained against her bra and teased his chest. She lifted her lips from his and looked up at him. "Maybe this should move to the bedroom?"

He smiled. "Go on upstairs and I'll make sure the alarm is set and door locked."

She nodded and briefly kissed his lips. Stepping out of his arms, she walked around him and up the stairs. She strolled into the bedroom and glanced out to the patio doors, cascading moonlight into her room. Charly sighed, thinking there seemed to be more stars out tonight in the sky. The bedroom door closed and strong arms wrapped around her waist.

Ethan's warm breath caressed the skin by her ear as he planted kisses along her neck. Her body ached in need and her nipples hardened. His one hand splayed across her stomach and pressed her back and bottom against the hard arousal in his pants. The other hand slipped between her denim-covered legs and reached for the part of her that was now humming in desire. His lips continued to caress down her neck and she lifted her arm to touch the soft strands of his hair.

The hand on her stomach reached up and made fast work of the buttons on her shirt. The soft cotton parted and his hand found her breast. Cupping it, he played the hard nipple between his fingers. She moaned and arched her back as his fingers teased the pressure to build across her belly. His hands came off her and, gently, he turned her to face him. "I'm glad you stayed," she whispered.

"I couldn't imagine not to," he breathed. The moonlight lit the room enough to accent the strong definitions of his face. She stepped back, slid her top off her shoulders, and made quick work of the rest of her clothes until she stood before him in her lace bra and thong. Charly closed the short distance between them and pulled his shirt up over his head before tossing it to the floor. Her hands slid over his skin, savoring the contoured strength of his muscles. His hands cupped her bottom and glided over her curves. His touch heightened every nerve in her body and made her hunger for more of him.

Quickly, she stripped him out of the remainder of his clothes and brought her body flush against him. His erection pressed against her skin and liquid desire pooled between her legs. He scooped her up in his arms and laid her carefully onto the bed. Her arms wrapped around his neck as his lips came to hers and his solid body pressed against her. His hard length teased her flesh and his tongue thrust in her mouth. Her nipples pushed hard against the lace of her bra and relished the heat of his chest. His tongue explored her mouth and entwined with hers. His large hands softly caressed over her. Eventually, his lips lifted from hers and started trailing down her neck.

He slid his hands around to her back and unfastened the clasp on her bra. As his hands slid from underneath her, he lifted the delicate lace from her breasts and tossed it to the side of the bed. Ethan's hot breath played across her skin, and soon, his tongue found one of her nipples. The tip of it grazed the taut peek and her back arched again in pleasure. His lips closed around it and he tenderly sucked as his tongue continued to taunt and tease.

She groaned as his lips came off her breast. The air of the room cooled it as his trail of kisses moved over her stomach and down to the top of her thong. His powerful body moved down hers, and his hands reached for the sides of the lace underwear. He quickly peeled them down and discarded them to the floor as well. Her legs fell shamelessly apart as his mouth worked down and the tip of his very talented tongue found her clit. Slowly, he moved over it and a finger traced over her wet folds. Her body shivered from the intensity of the pleasure building through her. His finger slid between the slick folds and then slid inside her.

Gasping, she brought her arms above her head. Her hands squeezed the pillow as his finger worked in and out of her, then a second finger joined the first. She whimpered as his tongue's flickering strokes picked up and her heart raced. Her breathing became irregular and her hips rose off the bed to his mouth. Ethan moaned against her sensitive flesh and her body bucked as she found release. His mouth clamped down and sent her even higher.

His wet lips and tongue trailed back up over her stomach and, eventually, to her mouth. She raised her head slightly as his head lowered. Charly tasted her climax on his tongue as his strong frame readjusted between her legs. He teased her wet folds, then pressed against them and thrust deep inside of her. He groaned against her tongue and her arms snaked around his neck. Resting her head against the pillow again, she pulled him harder to her breasts.

His rhythmic strokes started slow, then gradually picked up speed. She lifted her hips and met his plunges full on. His speed picked up and her legs wrapped around his waist. He gave a feral groan and thrust harder and deeper. His head lifted from hers and a wail of pleasure left her. Her wet walls squeezed tight around his solid length. A growl left Ethan and his release pumped hot and steady into her.

He buried his face in her hair and she held him close as she struggled with air herself. "I could get use to this," he whispered in her ear, then placed a soft kiss on her cheek. Charly continued to struggle to get her lungs functioning and couldn't agree more. The problem was, the more time she spent with Ethan, the more time she wanted with him. Would she ever get enough?

JT Schultz

## Chapter Nine

Ethan walked into the house he shared with his mom at close to eleven in the morning. She was in the kitchen having a coffee and lowered her mug to look at him. "I couldn't help but notice that you didn't come home last night. I thought you might be working."

Sighing, he stepped over to the table where she had papers scattered and sat down. "No, I didn't work. I was actually with a friend."

"How is Cole?" his mother asked with a lift of her brows. She genuinely liked his officer friend, but seriously questioned what was wrong with him since he was still single. So did Ethan, but she chalked it up to loving his mom and not finding a girl like her. In truth, she had nothing nice to say about anyone he dated.

"I wasn't with Cole. I was with Charly."

"I don't recall you mentioning a Charly. Is that a new firefighter at the station?" she asked, and looked at him from over her coffee mug.

*Tread carefully. Tread very, very carefully.*

"No, actually, she is a really great lady with a little girl. She lives right across the street from Mrs. Newman."

"Oh that Charly." She offered up a weak smile. "Mrs. Newman was telling me that she is just delightful and her little girl comes to visit her when she's outside on her porch."

"Her daughter's name is Leigh. She's a cutie."

"Mrs. Newman has said nothing but good things about both of them. I guess she always has messages from God for her and she always takes time to listen." She set her mug down and frowned. "So, you spent the night with her?"

"I'm thirty-two, not sixteen. Can we forego the premarital sex speech?" He got up, leaned in, and kissed her cheek, then walked over to the fridge. "So, what's on your agenda for today?"

"I have a meeting at the church for the society and then I have my Scrabble night with Betty and Patricia."

Ethan grabbed bottled water and walked back over to the table, but stayed standing.

His mother took off her glasses and set them down. "Will you be home for dinner?"

"Probably not. I promised Leigh I would go over and watch her new cartoon movie with her tonight." He furrowed his brows. "I haven't been around much here or spent much time with you as of late."

His mother smiled. "That's okay, I got busy at the nursing home with Betty and I figured you must be doing something important."

He sighed. "Actually, Mom, Charly is becoming important fast. I adore her and Leigh both."

"Well, I'm glad. Anything has to be an improvement over your last girlfriend."

There were so many things he could say to that remark, but decided not voice any of them. "Charly and Leigh are great, and I can hardly wait for you to meet them."

His mother smiled. "I'd like that." She stood and walked over to the sink, rinsed her mug, and put it in the dishwasher. She dried her hands and turned to Ethan. Her head tilted and she narrowed her gaze on him as she leaned against the counter. "You look good, in need of a shave, but you look good." She stepped closer to him. "You look relaxed. You know, I think I like the effect this girl has on you. Maybe she and Leigh would like to come to church on Sunday?"

Ethan unscrewed the cap on the bottled water and took a sip. "I'm not sure, I can ask."

"You work late that day, so I thought maybe you would keep me company."

Again, the urge to comment was extreme. "I'll think about it." He sighed. "I'll ask if she wants to go."

"From what I have heard about her, she might surprise you." His mother paused. "I just thought it would be nice. I'm the only one my age that doesn't have grandchildren."

*Oh hell! Not this again. If she liked anyone I went out with then I could change that, but when she goes after every woman with criticism, it makes any relationship hard, let alone having a child.*

"I'll keep it in mind." He drank his water and prevented himself from commenting further.

"Such a good boy." She reached for her coat that was over the back of the chair and smiled. "You have a good day and maybe a nice night." She slipped her coat on, patted his cheek, and hurried toward the door. When it shut, he released a breath he had been holding and shook his head. He glanced at the papers on the table and noticed a list of artists. He couldn't resist and pulled the sheet out. He read the names on the hand written list and noticed Joey Sinn at the top.

"What is it about you, Joey, that has everyone talking about you?" He could always ask Charly about her, but he didn't want to appear that he lived under a rock. Ethan could easily find out from another gallery. He set his water on the counter and removed his cell phone from his pocket. After running a search for galleries, he started calling them. They had all heard of Joey Sinn and all wished they had something of hers. Finally, he tried the last one, also the farthest away.

"Joey Sinn," the older gentleman said. "Yes, I have one piece from her. It's quite extraordinary. Shall I reserve it for you, sir?"

"Yes, I'd like to see it."

"It's not an actual painting, but a print."

"That's fine," Ethan answered, and ripped the page out of the phone book. "I'm on my way now. "Put it on hold for Ethan. I'll be there as soon as traffic allows."

"Very good, sir. I'll see you soon."

He ended the call and shook his head. This was insane. Why did he have to see this artist's work? He'd never noticed art before. Well, he had, he just didn't care about it. However, it was important to Charly, so he might as well see what the hottest commodity was. At least then he would have something to talk about with her. Not that they were lacking now, but at least he would come across more well-rounded.

It took him less than an hour to pull up to the gallery and walk in. "Hi," he greeted. "I called about the Joey Sinn print."

The elderly gentleman nodded and lifted up the picture. Ethan's head went back slightly in shock. His eyes widened. There, beneath a street lamp, was a couple wrapped in passion. His hand was on her breast over her blouse and her legs were wrapped around his waist. It was more than obvious what they were doing. The man's head was thrown back in bliss, and the woman looked completely satiated. Despite what the picture represented, it wasn't explicit; in fact, it was really quite nice with the colors and the capturing of a park. The more he stared at it, the more he liked it. He noticed the pencil mark in the corner. It was a scribbled JS.

He knew immediately this was the picture that Bryce wanted to get for his sister. Ethan understood why the artist was so popular. "I'll take it."

"No one can resist Joey Sinn. She brings fantasy to life. Let me ring that up for you. How will you be paying?"

"That depends, how much is it?" Ethan reached into his pocket and pulled out his wallet.

"Eight hundred and seventy-five dollars."

Ethan looked up and blinked. "You're kidding me?"

"The lady isn't cheap," the older man told him, chuckling.

Laughing, Ethan pulled out his credit card. "No, she isn't, but like my mother always said, the best girls aren't."

"Your mother sure has that right."

And she would detest that picture. "Do you take Visa?"

Charly was happy the gallery was shaping up nicely. In fact, it had filled out quickly and looked more like a place of business rather than an empty commercial space. She liked the shade of blue she had gone with. The black shelves and pedal stools gave the room a very striking look. Once she got creative and filled it, it would look fantastic. Her canvas had arrived and the construction crew had hung it on the wall for her. It had barely cleared the door at the back, and it was a larger door. The canvas was an amazing five feet by seven feet. The only question now was what to put on it that would satisfy Kendra Kensington's two hundred and fifty thousand dollars. The floor was the only thing left to do and it was still a little damp from the sprinklers the other day.

Her door opened and a distinguished older woman walked into the gallery. She paused and glanced around. She smiled at Charly and stepped closer. She was carrying a book, but Charly was relieved to see that, unlike Mrs. Newman, it wasn't a Bible. "I'm sorry, we're not open yet," she greeted as the woman's eyes fell to the canvas.

"Is that one a snow storm, or a bad fog?" she asked with a sparkle in her pretty blue eyes.

Laughing lightly, Charly shook her head. "It's neither. It actually is a blank canvas," Charly answered, and walked toward it.

"A picture is worth a thousand words, they say. My guess, that would be several thousand words and dollars," the woman replied, walking over next to her.

"It could be." She turned to the woman and smiled. "I'm sorry, can I help you?"

"Yes, I was looking for the owner. Is he in?" the woman asked with a smile.

"Actually, he isn't. There is no he. I'm the owner. And you are?"

"My name is Ruth. Here is a brochure for you." She pulled out a folded flyer and passed it to Charly. "I am with SAINT, the Society Against Inappropriate Naked Things."

*Holy hell! Not good.*

"I already donate to Breast Cancer and Pediatric AIDS Society. Thank you for considering me, though." She passed the flyer back out to the woman, who glanced at it and then smiled weakly.

"I'm not here for a donation. I'm here to express our concerns for some of the pieces of work you might have a mind to carry. What will be the name of the gallery?" She removed a pen from a rope around her neck and left the lid to dangle. She propped it and was ready to write.

"The Passionate Pleasures."

The woman started to write, then stopped mid-ink stroke. "Passionate, as in passion, and pleasures, as in sinful things?"

Charly smiled. "Just like." She folded her arms across her chest and waited. The lady looked stunned. It would wear off in a moment. It always did. She silently started ticking off the seconds in her head.

"I see. Well, this is the sort of thing that SAINT is concerned about."

"I'm sorry to hear that."

"You seem like a nice girl; I knew you would understand." She hauled out another piece of paper and passed it to her. "These are the artists that we have taken a stand against."

Looking at the top of the list, she blinked at the first name and skimmed the list. She knew over half the artists, and guessed that the others were local. "I know a lot of these artists and had planned on carrying a few of them."

"Well, that wouldn't be in your best interest," the woman told her crisply.

"Some of these artists fetch several thousands of dollars per piece. I notice Joey Sinn at the top of the list. Do you have any idea what some of her work sells for?"

Ruth's lips thinned into a line. "No, nor do I care to. She is a tool of the devil. Her paintbrush does nothing but stroke sin and debauchery."

Flinching, Charly stepped back and blinked at the woman in front of her. "Wow, debauchery. Do you even know what that word means? Do you even know anything about art?" Charly stepped closer to the woman. "Let me clarify. Joey Sinn's work portrays pleasure, ecstasy, and bliss. It comes across as sinful to those that are closed-minded and possibly lacking in their own sexual fulfillment."

The woman gasped. "I have never—"

"I already concluded that by your attitude." She crumpled the piece of paper and set it on the clipboard. "Thank you for stopping by, and I'll be sure to take this conversation into account."

Stepping back, the woman re-clipped her pen to the lid and hugged her clipboard tight. "I'm not done with you. I hope you know that SAINT holds a lot of clout in this community, and I refuse to have brazen, sexually explicit things and all sorts of nakedness tarnishing this community's good name."

"And I refuse to have a society that can't see past their self-righteousness stop me from earning a living and giving to the community art that will give them joy. You walked in through the door. I suggest you walk back out of it. Thanks for stopping by, and next time you're in the neighborhood, keep walking and don't come in."

"I've had enough of your tongue-in-cheek attitude, missy. I am far from through with you and I will do everything in my power to see that this place of depravity never opens."

"Get out of my gallery, and if you threaten me again, I'll call the police. Leave, before I change my mind and call them now."

"You're going to hell, working the devil's magic," she tossed venomously, and walked to the door. She paused, turned, and scowled.

"On the bright side, at least in hell, I will not be with the likes of your closed-minded and open-mouthed self-righteousness." Charly smiled and waved. "On a positive note, have a nice a day and God bless."

Glowering in anger, the woman pushed on the door. "I will stop you." She walked over the threshold and Charly exhaled.

It was all she could do not to run over and lock the door. If Cole had his way, it would be. The man had almost driven her insane this morning going over every detail with her and the locksmith. He had asked her more about her paintings and she had failed to answer him. Failed was the wrong word; she had avoided answering any questions that might reveal Joey Sinn. Liz had called her once and Jenna twice to make sure that she'd kept her alias safe. She sighed and glanced up at the canvas. Her cell phone rang, and she walked over to the large, black counter and picked up the device.

"Hello, Joey Sinn."

"Joey, darling, thank heavens," Kendra droned from the other end of the line. "I just wanted to let you know that I received Charly's invitation for the gallery opening today in the mail and I will most definitely be there. Now, about my painting, have you come up with something brilliant yet?"

*Don't even think of lying*, the angel on her shoulder warned. *Lie, lie, lie, we are talking two hundred and fifty thousand dollars*, the devil chided.

"I have, and I think it'll be marvelous." *And now I'm officially going to hell. At least Ruth won't be there.*

191

"Oh, Joey! Thank you." She made kiss sounds and Charly shook her head. "Okay this is what I am going to do. I am going to send you a small part of the money, a mere token really. I will send it in care of Charly at the gallery. I think you should feel inspired with a check for say thirty-five thousand."

*That's inspirational.* "That would be wonderful, Kendra, thank you. "

"I just can't think of my favorite artist falling into the starving category and being forced to get a normal job."

"Thank you again, Kendra. I'll make sure that the picture is hot and worthy."

"I have always lusted for a man in uniform, any uniform. I used to think up the most erotic fantasies with all sorts of men in uniform. Blatantly, I love policeman, fireman, navy, marines. Hell, I'd settle for a highway patrolman as long as he wore his hat."

*Her money is going to be covering my counseling appointments.* "I'll keep it in mind."

"I knew you would understand me. You take care, and may the paintbrush be with you." She ended the call and Charly pulled the phone away from her ear to stare at it. She closed the phone and shook her head. "I don't understand you, Kendra, but I do understand your money." She set the phone down, headed to her office, and grabbed the bucket of primer for the canvas, as well as a roller.

She brought them out and realized that she needed the ladder from the back. She glanced to the door and hurried back to the large bay area. The cans of paint and shelves were now gone, but paint still marked the cement from where it had spilled and exploded. She grabbed the ladder and carried it out front. She wasn't really dressed for painting, but her denim skirt and sweater weren't exactly new either. If she could prep the canvas; it would save time later. She quickly applied a coat and moved the ladder to take in the canvas when the door opened. The smell of his cologne reached her nose before she even turned and smiled. "What are you doing here?"

He laughed wickedly. "I thought I would surprise you."

Ethan took in Charly's appearance. She looked beautiful and radiant. She had a white color of paint in her hair and on the side of her cheek, but looked incredible. Most of all, she looked happy to see him. "Miss me?"

"I did," she admitted as he stepped closer. "Actually, could you lock the door?"

He glanced to the door, stepped back, and locked it. He looked back at her as he walked forward. "Shouldn't it have been locked before I arrived?"

"Yes, but let's not tell Officer Skippy, okay?"

His one brow arched and his arms reached out for her. They circled her waist and he chuckled. "You must be referring to my buddy Cole." He drew her in a tighter hold and grinned. "As I recall, you two didn't hit it off very well."

"No, and it didn't get better until after I turned down his proposal and murmured your name."

"I think things improved for me and you shortly thereafter."

She slipped her arms around his neck and nodded. "I wouldn't trade that. Now, are you just going to look sexy, or are you going to kiss me?"

"And there is that wonderful bluntness."

She frowned and winced. "I had a horrible day with a very dislikeable person, and my bluntness actually took hold. It was ugly, but she was so rude."

He leaned in and kissed her lips lightly. "It's often hard to deal with rude people. Some people don't know when they should just keep quiet."

"As was the case this time. I feel bad; I don't usually get impolite."

"I know, sweetheart." He kissed her lips again. "I think you should just push the horrible encounter from your mind and think of how incredible this encounter could be." He kissed her lips lightly again and glanced around. "Charly, this place is looking great. Have you come up with a name for it yet?" He released her for the moment and took in the room. It was trendy, but held a certain ambiance that was classy.

"I have, I was thinking Passionate Pleasures."

Ethan turned and grinned. "I like it and think that would be great. So, will you be carrying a lot of pleasure pleasing artwork? I hear Joey Sinn is very popular."

Her eyes narrowed on him and her look turned not only thoughtful, but pleased. "I thought you weren't into art."

"I'm learning as I go," he confessed with a chuckle.

"Ah, a work in progress."

Chuckling again, he nodded and placed his hands on his hips. "Something like that. Bryce, one of my men, was trying to locate a Joey Sinn print and I went and picked up one for him today. He was pleased."

"Oh, Ethan, you should have said something. I'm sure I could have helped." Her brows dipped and genuine curiosity animated her features. "You must be referring to the 'Pleasure in the Park' — it's the only one of hers that has prints and limited quantities."

"That sounds like the right title for this piece. It was incredible. I can see why the artist is so successful." It was true. Bryce had been thrilled about the print, but not so much as to the bill he owed. However, when he had phoned his sister and heard her happiness, he told Ethan it was worth every penny and would pay him back when they got paid. Ethan wasn't worried about it. "Why are you looking at me like that?"

"Next time, just come to see me. It's a great painting. The original sold for just about eleven thousand dollars. There were only a thousand prints made. You were lucky to get one." She laughed and shook her head.

Ethan blinked. "Eleven thousand? Wow, am I ever in the wrong line of work. Joey Sinn must be making a killing."

Her features lost some of their sparkle. "That she is." She turned away and walked toward the canvas. Ethan took in her long, tanned legs beneath her skirt and his groin stiffened.

He stepped over to Charly and reached for her. Placing his hands on her hips, he pulled her in next to him and grinned. "You look good. I think you look sexy with paint on you and that creative sparkle in your eye."

"And you're not only sexy, but charming," she whispered, and tilted her head up slightly. Her lashes fluttered closed and Ethan lowered his lips to hers. She tasted great and her mouth opened. His tongue took the invite and sought out hers. She met the kiss with a hunger of desire.

His hands slid from her hips and around to her ass. He pressed her against the now throbbing ache in his pants and she moaned softly. Her hands slid to his shoulders and ran down his arms, then back up to slide over the front of his chest. Despite the layers of clothes, his skin flamed from her caresses.

He wanted her and knew that there was no way they were going to leave there without him having her. This may be their only chance to have sex in the gallery and he wasn't going to miss it. He deepened the kiss and gently dropped his hands to the silky flesh of her legs. She whimpered a sigh and pressed her pelvis against his arousal. Knowing she wanted him to, he eased her back a little further and stopped when they reached the wall. He slid his hands over her legs and pushed up the denim.

Her lips lifted from his and his eyes opened. "I'm against the canvas."

He couldn't stop the grin. "I wasn't paying attention. I'm sorry, it's wet."

Her tongue slid across her lower lip, then rose to her top one. She looked hotter than hell, and that sultry look alone was almost his undoing. "It's not any wetter than I am," she replied and, with a quick grasp to his wrist, he led his hand to the very damp spot of fabric and skin between her legs.

Ethan groaned and his fingers slipped in around the soft lace and caressed her folds. Her hands slid to his belt buckle and made quick work of his zipper. She slid her hand underneath the hem of his shirt and she gently touched his skin. He was more than aroused and slipped his finger into her. She gasped and caressed his erection. He moaned at the feathery strokes, and was even more surprised when she pulled her hand off him from under his clothes and tugged at the sides of his jeans. In that simple move, she yanked down his pants and he sprung free, hard and ready for her.

Her hand resumed its light touches and he moved his fingers from between her legs and brought both hands to the sides of her thong. He gave the delicate fabric a nudge and it dropped to the floor. Her hand stopped its gentle rubbing and she slid her arms around his neck. Ethan slipped his hands around to her bare bottom and gently lifted her up. Her legs wrapped around his waist and the tip of him pressed against her folds and slid into her tight, wet walls.

Moaning, he claimed her lips and balanced her against the wet canvas. He thrust in slow and deliberate. He brought a soft moan of pleasure to her with every movement. He picked up speed and her legs tightened around his waist. She pulled her lips from his and placed wet, hot kisses on his neck by his ear. He thrust harder, and in this position, he wasn't sure how long he would last. She felt incredible, and his erection throbbed, wanting release. Her inside walls clamped tight around him and she whimpered in pleasure as she found release.

He slammed into her and he climaxed. Charly wrapped her arms tighter around him and ran her nose over the heated skin below his ear. Ethan groaned as his orgasm pulsed more inside her. He cupped her head gently and felt the wet paint in it. He didn't pull away. With her butt against the canvas and her legs still circling him, he kissed her cheek. There was so much he wanted to say to her. Nothing he said would describe how he felt. Well, one thing would, but it was way to too soon to say it.

JT Schultz

## Chapter Ten

The last four days had flown by at a rampant speed and Charly was unsure where they'd gone. She smiled as she thought about the sex at the gallery. It had taken almost an hour to get the paint off her in the shower after that encounter. Then again, it would have gone faster if they hadn't stopped to have sex. Thankfully, they were smarter these days, making sure that the door was shut to the smoke alarm when venturing into any activity that would create steam.

Ethan was back to work and on nights. As she sat in the chair in her room, she hated to admit that she missed him. However, with him at work, she had plenty of time to paint. She had painted up a storm and had filled several orders. Part of her felt guilty for not telling him about her alias, Joey Sinn; the other part of her knew that she couldn't risk it. Joey Sinn's popularity seemed to be growing.

Unfortunately, so were her creepy notes and love letters from her stalker and her rounds with Ruth from SAINT. The woman was becoming her nemesis. She had stopped by again today to threaten that she would do whatever it took to shut Charly down. When she asked for Charly's name, Charly told her in less than ladylike terms where to go and had picked up her cell phone to call Cole. The woman had retreated, less than happy, and Charly's mood had soured completely.

She still hadn't painted anything on the canvas at the gallery, but some of that was because of the debate to reorder a new one. Her escapade of debauchery, as Ruth would have called it, with Ethan had slightly dented it.

Glancing down at the sketchbook in her lap, she sighed and heard a sound downstairs. Her heart picked up speed and she froze. Her house phone rang; a tremor of fear ran through her body. She picked up the cordless phone and stared at the number. It was Ethan's cell phone. "Hello?"

"Hey, sweetheart, what are you doing?"

She sighed in relief and heard a sound downstairs again. Terror tickled across her skin and down her spine. "I'm up in the room sketching. Ethan, there's a noise downstairs."

"I know. I thought I'd call you and warn you I left early tonight. Jim is arguing with his wife's mother, so he decided to come in. That way I could be here with you. I didn't want to frighten you. I have the key you gave me."

She sighed. "That was sweet of Jim."

"Yeah, I guess he and his mother-in-law don't exactly get along, and since she's there for another week and a half, he thought he'd escape." The sound of the door shutting echoed from the phone and from downstairs.

She heard the deadbolt turn over and then punching, which meant Ethan was resetting the alarm.

"Well, I'm glad you decided to come here," she told him, and heard his steps coming up the stairs.

"What can I say? You're the first person I want to see when I wake up." He walked in through the door of the bedroom and grinned. "You look beautiful and I'm glad I came here to see it."

She giggled and hung up the phone. Ethan lowered his and he stepped over to the ottoman where her legs were. He frowned slightly and touched the white cotton shirt. "This looks like mine?" His fingers touched the collar.

"It is. Remember, I removed it off you this morning. Only it smelled like your cologne and, well—"

Ethan slid up on the ottoman and leaned in to her. "You're such a romantic." He glanced at the sketchpad. Even under the faint, soft light on the table next to the phone, he looked sexy. "The house smells like acrylic and now I catch you in the act with the sketchpad. Can I peek?"

"No," she told him, and slid her bottom forward on the chair. "Not until you kiss me."

"I can do that," he whispered, and lowered his mouth to hers. Her hand not holding the pencil cupped his cheek and she relished the moment. His lips were cool, but his tongue warm as he teased it against hers. She opened her mouth and met his tongue with her own as it slid in to explore. Her nipples hardened and his hands slipped to her waist. He tasted terrific and felt even better. She dared to think she was falling in love with him and when he kissed her as deeply as he was doing right now, something inside her knew he felt the same way.

He lifted his lips from hers. She opened her eyes and blinked at him. "What are you thinking?"

"I'm thinking that if that kiss had continued, I would've taken you here, but I think that, since I've had to work the last couple nights, I would rather have you in bed than in the chair. However, this will be reserved for another time."

Giggling, she nodded. "I hope so. I'm glad you're here."

"Me too," he whispered, and kissed her lips lightly. He got up off the ottoman and started to undress. Charly left the nightstand light on and stepped over to the bed where she flopped on the heavy duvet. She watched as he stripped down and took in every perfectly cut sinew. His body was perfection, an artist's dream, and her most erotic pleasure. He walked over to the bed and she noticed he was already stiffening. His desire for her was unreal and she basked in it. She climbed under the covers, as he did, and picked up her sketchpad.

"Now that we are comfortable, I want to look."

She nodded and passed it to him willingly. He flipped it so that it was at the beginning. It was a new sketchbook and most of them were of him. He truly was the inspiration that she had needed to get the creative juices flowing.

"Well, I certainly know who my biggest fan is," he teased gently. He glanced up at her. "You're so talented."

"And you are so incredibly sexy. How could I not sketch you? Hell, I'll dedicate the whole book to you."

His smile stole her breath and he glanced back down at the sketchbook. His brows furrowed and he tilted it to look at something in the corner. Her heart slammed to a stop. She knew what he was looking at. He sat in bed and glanced around the room, then rested his gaze back at her. His expression was unreadable. He looked back down at the sketch. "JS." He shook his head and then turned toward her.

She sat up and pulled her lip between her bottom teeth. "Ethan—"

"I've seen initials done just like that on the print I bought for Bryce." He swallowed hard and his Adam's apple rose then fell. "You're Joey Sinn?"

She closed her eyes and nodded as a pang of guilt hit her full force. Slowly, she opened them again and gazed at him. "Liz and Jenna are the only ones who know. Of course and the crazed stalker knows, who is actually a very obsessed fan."

"Oh God," he whispered, and shook his head. His body tensed up and he eased back from her. "Unbelievable." He glanced around the room. "It certainly explains how you can afford things. You certainly aren't the starving artist, are you?"

She wasn't sure she liked his reaction. "No." Her voice was softer than a whisper. "I wanted to tell you, Ethan. I just didn't know how."

He nodded once and closed the book, gently tossing it to the floor along with the pencil, then he stood. He started pacing the floor, shaking his head. "So, you're the mysterious Joey Sinn. I have no clue what to say."

Self-doubt and insecurity built within her and a sudden uneasiness had settled in the air between them. "I think anything would do at this point."

"How about...I think you definitely are worth every penny and I couldn't be more proud. Of course, not everyone is going to agree with that." He scrubbed his hands over his handsome face then rested his gaze on her. "In fact, some people are going to hate your work and be downright verbal and opinionated about it."

She right away thought of SAINT and the wretched woman who insisted on darkening her gallery doorway. Charly studied Ethan and couldn't understand why he suddenly wore such a torn expression. "Are you mad?"

"No, I'm not really even surprised." He frowned slightly. "Charly, could your stalker be someone who doesn't approve of your work? Because you know there will be many others who have a problem with it."

Her heart filled with a fleeting moment of fear. "Do you have a problem with it?"

Silence.

The longer the quiet stretched, the more she questioned what they were doing, and if this was even going to work between them. Why had she even opened herself up to rejection? Right, because she had thought he was different. "Maybe you should go think about things."

An unreadable emotion flickered across his face. "No, I don't have a problem with your work as Joey Sinn." He stepped closer to the bed again and smiled weakly. "I just worry how other people will react if and when they find out."

He climbed back onto the bed and caressed a hand through her hair. He stared at her as if seeing her for the first time. Though his words were reassuring, something in his tone revealed minor hesitation. Maybe he just needed time to adjust to the news. Maybe.

She blinked and decided to ask the question again, that way there were no misunderstandings. "Are you sure you don't have a problem with my work?"

"No, because I've experienced your passion firsthand." He inched closer to her. "I am, however, more turned on, I think, than I have ever been."

Exhaling a breath, relief washed over her, though part of her wasn't totally convinced. "I think I can help you with that."

"You sure as the hell better." He chuckled and reached for her, sliding his naked body over her. His length was rock hard and his body warm. His hands skimmed over her and one dropped between her legs. She spread her thighs and savored his touch. "You are so wet and not wearing panties," he moaned, and slid up her body. He repositioned himself between her legs and worked the buttons undone on the shirt. The fabric fell open and the air of the room fanned her bare breasts.

His mouth planted kisses and his tongue licked one taut nipple and then the other. He worked between the two, sucking and teasing one as his fingers played with the other. Pressure tightened in her belly and she almost climaxed right then. Her back arched and she whimpered as his erection slid against the soft flesh of her leg. Ethan's lips covered hers and the tip of his arousal played in her wet folds. He thrust deep into her and her body slightly trembled.

He groaned against her mouth and moved slowly in and out of her. He found a steady rhythm and picked up speed. Her hips rose to his thrusts and he pulled his lips from hers. His chest weighed down against her breasts and his elbows dug into the mattress. His thrusts picked up speed and moved her whole body. She felt the familiar twitching as the pressure built across her stomach again. "God, Ethan!" she cried as her pussy squeezed around him. He thrust hard and a feral groan left him as his release emptied inside of her. She wrapped her arms around his neck and lifted her lips to his. She gently kissed him as they struggled for breath.

"I think you need to get off early and come home more often." She thought for a moment. This wasn't his home, technically, but it sure felt like it.

"I think so too, especially if this is what it gets me." He kissed her lips briefly and his expression became serious. "I'll never tell your secret, Charly. Not even to Cole."

She smiled and fought for air. "I know."

Ethan found it was a slow night at work, and after the day Charly had experienced with another onslaught of black envelopes, he had hated leaving her. He was almost tempted to call in someone to replace him and surprise her by going home early like the last night.

Home.

That's where he had certainly laid his jeans on the floor lately. It felt right. Maybe that's because he was head over heels in love with her and Leigh both. It was obvious Charly looked at him as a part of her house. It was home because, right now, that was exactly where he wanted to be.

Liz and Jenna swore they would keep Charly and Leigh company. He had only felt a little better when Jason had called on his way home from ball practice to say he would swing by and hang out with the ladies. Still, under the circumstances, Ethan wished he could be with her tonight.

"Ethan!" Tony called to him. "Something's not right over at the gallery."

He hated the way that sounded.

"Is there some reason your mother should be there?"

He dropped the wrench to the cement floor and stepped from behind the fire truck to the front bay door of the station. He stood next to

Tony as Bryce moved over to them. The last thing he needed was his mother talking to Charly and finding out that she was Joey Sinn. Other than her friends, Ethan was the only one that knew.

"I haven't seen Charly over there all afternoon," Bryce told them. Neither had Ethan. A strange man he didn't recognize flew out of the gallery.

"Hey!" he called out, and started down the driveway. Tony and Bryce were close behind. He hit the sidewalk as the gallery windows blew out in a puff of smoke. Ethan dropped to the ground and shielded his face.

"Let's get over there!" he yelled, and reached for his cell phone on his hip. "Cole, it's Ethan. I need you to get Charly. There's a fire at the gallery." He slammed his phone shut, headed to his fire retardant clothes, and knew that this was going to crush her. Her work and her dreams were gone in a flicker. The gallery opening was just over a week away. This was going to destroy her opening on time. He would have to plan something extra special for her to help with this setback.

Bryce threw on the siren and pulled out of the drive. He turned the wheel and brought the hose close to the building. Everything seemed to happen in slow motion and he remembered the paints and paint remover in the back bay area. Thankfully, the guys were aware. He slowed and heard the sirens in the distance. He had never gone to a fire with this much emotional attachment and felt lost. The sprinkler system had prevented it from getting too out of control, but it was still a charred mess. He motioned to Bryce he was leaving, swearing that if he didn't throw up it would be a miracle.

He exited into the night and stepped onto the street. He watched Cole's police cruiser pull up and Charly jumped out. He hurried over to her. She fought past the officers, slapping their hands as she crossed the line. Ethan pulled off his helmet and his mask and tossed them to the ground. His arms came out and she threw herself at him. He circled his arms around her and she started to cry. Liz and Jason pulled up and studied what remained of the gallery. He glanced over to Cole, who shook his head and wore a defeated expression. Bryce walked over to him and started talking to him, but he couldn't make out what his friend was saying. They all knew how much this had meant to her and everything she had lost. He was going to kill the person who did this.

"Charly, sweetheart," he soothed, then remembered Tony asking about his mother. An alarm went off in his head and he gently pulled her off of him a bit. She looked up at him, her face streaked with ash and tears running down her cheeks.

Her hands came up and cupped his face. "You're alive. I was so scared." Terror marked her pretty features.

"Sweetheart, the gallery." How did he tell her the damage was severe?

She glanced to the charred store front and shook her head. "You're safe." She glanced down at his outfit and fresh tears fell down her cheeks.

Pulling off his gloves, he took them and tossed them down. His hands came up and wiped the tears away from her face. "I do this for a living, remember?"

She sniffled hard and slowly nodded. "It's just that..."

He could tell what she was going to say by the look in her eyes. "I love you too, sweetheart. I do."

"I love you, and I was scared."

Ethan wrapped his arms around her and hugged her close to him. She seemed more worried about him then the gallery. Cole walked over to him and he noticed his mother standing nearby. Charly pulled out of his arms and glanced to Cole. Her gaze fell to his mother and her body stiffened. This was not a good time for them to meet.

"Ethan, what are you doing?" his mother demanded, catching him completely off guard. She cast a scowl to Charly. Her eyes then fell back on Ethan. "I certainly hope you don't handle all your fires this way."

"You psychotic bitch," Charly yelled, and glared at his mom. "I bet you're reveling in this moment. "You swore to me just yesterday that you would go out of your way to stop me from opening this gallery. You threatened on more than one occasion. How could a SAINT such as yourself go this far?" Charly was pure hostility.

*Oh hell!*

"You're going to let this little whore speak to me like this?"

Ethan was stunned. "Mom, Charly. Charly, this is my mother, Ruth Valiant."

Charly gasped, pulled her gaze off his mom, and turned to him in horror. "This is the woman that has caused me nothing but grief?" Her body started to tremble and she stepped around him to stare at the gallery.

Ethan's head was reeling. Not only was Charly opening the gallery, she was the infamous Joey Sinn. Not good for anyone concerned. He knew the night he found out that his mother and Charly would never get a long and they would never agree. This was a new form of hell.

Cole walked over to him with a bleak look. He turned to Ethan's mother. "Mrs. Valiant, can you explain to me please why there are witnesses that are placing you at the gallery before the explosion?"

*Oh, God, Mom. This is not happening.*

He turned to Charly, who walked slowly toward the gallery. It wasn't safe, but with the fire out, there was no immediate danger. Her shoulders shook and he knew she was crying. His heart broke. He turned back to Cole and his mother. His mom was getting hostile, but not answering Cole's questions. He tried to tune into the conversation, but his mind wouldn't let him. His heart ached and confusion was drowning him. He knew where this was headed and he didn't like it. Ethan would have to choose between the woman he truly cared about and his mom.

He glanced back and saw Charly standing in front of the canvas where he had made love to her. He walked over to where she stood and came to a stop. Her gaze never left the canvas. She just stared at it. Ethan's mouth parted in surprise. It was practically unscathed by the flames and had nothing but smoke and most likely water damage. He glanced around the rest of the room. It was destroyed, yet that canvas was, for the most part, unharmed.

Her long lashes blinked and she continued to stare at it as if it was the only thing in the world. "It was supposed to be a painting for one of Joey's clients."

"Charly."

She turned and stared at him. Her pretty face was void of all emotion, the expression as catatonic as her voice. "The lady was going to pay me two hundred and fifty thousand dollars."

Ethan blinked and shook his head. "I don't think I heard you, because for a moment it sounded like you said two hundred and fifty thousand."

"I did." Her expression never wavered. "It doesn't matter now. Your mother, the one I called a psycho bitch, she won. For the record, I wouldn't have called her that if I'd known she was your mom." She looked back at the wall.

"Sweetheart."

Charly's expression became bleak and her full lips thinned. "Don't call me that. I know how much you love your mom and I won't come between you." She never even looked at him. Her voice still held no fleck of emotion. "I won't even press charges against her if she is guilty for her righteous dominion and preventing me from opening the gallery."

Her words were cool, but it was her lack of emotion that slowly killed him. "What are you saying, Charly?"

She turned and looked at him. "Go to your mother, Ethan. She needs you."

He couldn't believe this. "Just like that, it's done?"

"There is no option." Her voice was wavering. "You told me you wouldn't let anyone hurt me. You can't stop your mother; she has done more damage than you'll ever know."

"Charly, no one knows you're Joey Sinn."

"And I choose to have it that way."

Frustration overruled every other emotion coursing through his body. "You can't keep living a double life. We can't protect you —"

"A double life?" She blinked at him with contempt, "I don't need protecting, Ethan. I don't need anyone. Especially you if you think I'm living a lie."

He was frustrated. "I never said that."

"You may as well have." Her temper surfaced in the simple statement.

This wasn't how things were supposed to go. For a moment, his life had been great. "I just don't know if you painting stuff you can't put your name on is a great idea."

Disappointment washed over her pretty features. "No. I can tell. You know what, I asked you if you had a problem with me painting as Joey Sinn, you said you didn't. Then we had sex. So in my opinion, the only time you have a problem with it is if someone else knows the truth."

"Charly —"

"Save it Ethan. I don't have a problem with me; apparently you have a problem with me." Tears filled her eyes.

"I'm just saying that you doing what you're doing is now endangering your life." He shook his head and didn't know what else he could say to her. "You need to think about this unless you have a death wish!"

"Excuse me?"

"The stalker, the threat to your gallery. What's it going to be, your life or doing what you love?" Could the woman be anymore stubborn? What if she'd been in the gallery? He couldn't imagine.

A tear slipped down her cheek. "I don't love anything or anyone except for Leigh." Her tone held an undercurrent he didn't like. "Go to your mother. She needs you. I don't need to be around her after this, which means I can't be around you."

"Charly, please—"

She  glanced back at the wall. "I'll have Cole drop your stuff off to you. I won't ruin your relationship with your mother. There's no need to." She turned her body and stepped toward him. The urge to hold her was overwhelming, yet he restrained. "She wins. You win. I quit." Charly stepped around him and walked out of the gallery,  and quite possibly his life.

Charly was miserable. The mornings turned into days and she moved slowly and ached. She had wanted to throw in the towel and not continue. She could forget the gallery altogether, but her friends wouldn't let her. Even Cole was stopping by to check on her. Jacque had heard the news and had been a blessing, coming over with meals to take the chore off her. He had offered a shoulder to cry on more than once.

Raul the gardener must have had heard something because he, too, was stopping in regularly, and in the three days since the fire, she had experienced the familiar downpour of men. None of them, however, was Ethan. On the fourth day, she called the alarm company and the construction company and had them go back in and work. She was going to pull it together and move on. The only thing was, she had a huge hole in her heart from where Ethan had been and she ached to her core. She returned from the gallery and pulled into the driveway, knowing that Jenna was inside with Leigh. She jumped out of her truck and noticed Ethan's car in front of Mrs. Newman's. She closed her eyes and bit back the pain as Mrs. Newman's front door opened.

She hurried toward the walk; she didn't want to face Ethan. "Oh, Charly, how wonderful, dear." Mrs. Newman's voice rang out like a choir. Charly longed to pretend that she didn't hear her.

*Just keep walking. Let the old lady have her company*, the devil sneered with a huff. *Turn around and talk to her. She has always been sweet to you,* the angel scolded.

With an inward groan, Charly turned around and faced Mrs. Newman's front yard. *Double hell, Ethan and Ruth over there.* "Hi, Mrs. Newman," Charly called, trying to keep all nerves and hurt out of her tone. She was a businesswoman, she could fake cheerful.

"Charly, come over, dear. I have a message from the Lord for you."

*Now? Hell, why can't you just have him leave a message on my answering machine?*

She smiled and knew both Ethan and Ruth were watching her. She kept the plastered smile on her face and crossed the street to her sweet, yet often pain in the ass, elderly neighbor. "Yes, Mrs. Newman?" She made damn sure she didn't look at either Ethan or Ruth and her gaze stayed fixed on the woman with the message.

"You look tired, dear. Are you not sleeping? Please don't tell me you're working all the time again?"

Charly forced her smile broader. "Of course not. Now, you said you had a message?" Feeling the heat of Ethan's gaze on her, she forced herself not to cry. She stole a sideways glance to Ruth who was studying her, then focused on Mrs. Newman.

"Well, isn't that strange. I had it on the tip of my tongue a moment ago."

*Fantastic.*

"You know, the same thing happened to me on Sunday. I was getting ready for church and I put on my pink hat, which is just craziness because I never wear my pink hat to church."

Charly glanced to Ruth, who met her gaze and quickly looked away. She turned back to Mrs. Newman.

"Anyway, I took a look in the mirror, and even though I forgot that it had been Sunday, I realized that it was no big deal because I could wear that hat anywhere. I guess we sometimes have a way of doing things and we forget that we can wear a different hat and still have the same effect."

Her mouth fell open and she closed it quickly. How did Mrs. Newman do that? Deliver the most appropriate story at the oddest of times? Yet every time she did, it fit. Charly's lips twitched and she laughed lightly. "I think that's a great story, Mrs. Newman."

"You don't wear hats, do you, Charly?" the older woman asked.

"No, but you know, I might start wearing them more." She mustered up some bravery and glanced to Ethan. His eyes were sparkling and his lips curved slightly into a smile. They just stood there a minute. Then, all the pain of how much she missed him came flooding over her and her smile faded. The familiar prick behind her eyes started and knew she was going to cry. She snapped her attention off Ethan and focused on Mrs. Newman. "I have to go; we'll talk soon," she told her neighbor, and hurried away. Her heart broke as she crossed the street and ran into the house. She shut the door and slid down against it as she started to cry.

Jenna came out of the living room. "Oh, honey." She knelt down beside her and hugged her. "Don't cry, Charly."

"I still love him, Jenna. I don't think I'll ever stop." Charly stared at her friend and saw the worry in her eyes. "It doesn't matter what hat I wear. I can't have him back."

Jacque moved from around the corner and knelt down beside her. "Don't cry, *chérie.* Sometime things just take time."

"And sometimes they take cookies and ice cream," she stammered out between sobs.

"I bake for you," Jacque assured her, and kissed her cheek softly. "I will not be able to do it in my nakedness with the cookie cruncher in the house, but I shall bake for you."

"Great." She turned to Jenna and sniffed. "Get me a glass of wine, please, in the meantime?"

She nodded. "You could always try talking to him, Charly. Cole says he is pretty miserable." "I'm not surprised. I've met his mother." She burst into tears again and buried her face in her hands.

JT Schultz

## Chapter Eleven

Charly heaved a sigh and paced the floor. Tomorrow night was the opening of the gallery, her gallery, Passionate Pleasures. She glanced around. The extra overtime and hustle from the construction crew was incredible. There was no trace of the fire. Her friends had been supportive through it all and even Jacque had stayed the night of her meltdown. He had slept on the sofa and had left early in the morning. Cole was on top of the steady flow of black envelopes and twisted love letters from the crazed fan, and even stopped by nightly to check on her. Liz and Jason had spent a night in the guest room, worried for Charly and Leigh's safety.

She hadn't done much painting, but some. She had finally come clean with both Cole and Jason about her alias and had threatened them both to never breathe a word. Of course, Cole had reminded her it was against the law to utter threats. Thankfully, he'd laughed, most likely due to her look of death.

Charly had some great pieces from a couple artists locally and from across the country. Most dealt with the exotic side of life, or the erotic. She stared at the large canvas on the wall. Why the hell did the construction crew put it back up? Its edges were burnt and the smoke had marked it. So had she and Ethan in the midst of great sex. Her heart tugged, then tightened at the thought of him.

She turned away from the canvas and resumed her pace of the floor. Could anyone possibly be any more miserable? She highly doubted it. Charly tried not to think of how wonderful her life had been. After losing Ethan, she'd lost everything. Her muse hadn't surfaced, but she was sure it was riding around in Ethan's jeans. Not that she blamed the muse. He was something else, down to his very good-sized ladder.

"You're going to wear a spot on the floor," Cole told her, causing her to look over to where he and Jason were moving a marble statue. It was a remarkable piece of a couple in the throes of passion.

"You should be filling the canvas on the wall," Jason gently reminded.

"I know." She sighed and turned to the window. Slowly, she stepped closer and stared out. She sighed as she looked across the street to the fire station and noticed Ethan's car in the parking lot. Maybe she should just go over and tell him that she missed him.

"You know he isn't going to come over here, right?"

Charly turned again to Cole. She blinked and nodded. She walked over to the officer and smiled. He was gorgeous; so was Jason. She glanced to him as he stood by Cole and grabbed his bottled water off the sales counter. "I wish he would come over."

The two guys exchanged a look and she hung her head. "There is nothing that says you can't go see him, Charly."

She lifted her head and stared at Jason. He and Liz had turned out to be quite the item. If they could just stop having sex on her sofa, she would be happier. "And what? Tell him that I'm horribly miserable and I miss him so much that it hurts?"

The expressions on both guys' faces turned soft and sympathetic.

"Go over there and tell him that I don't know when it happened, but I did something totally stupid like fall in love with him and that I don't know if I'll ever paint again because he brought so much color to my life?" She closed her eyes. Warm tracks of hot tears slipped down her cheeks. Quickly, she lifted her hands and brushed them away.

"Being male, I would say that would work," Cole assured her. "Only I would leave out the part where falling in love with him is stupid. We can't choose who we fall in love with, Charly." He rolled his eyes and walked over to her. His strong frame wrapped her in a hug. He stepped back and put his fingers gently under her chin. "Every man that meets you loves you, honey. Only I think I know a man *in* love with you."

"Cole, I'm not marrying you."

Jason chuckled and she looked around Cole to scowl at him. "Not Cole, Ethan. Drag that sinful ass over there and tell him how you feel." He shook his head. "I would definitely use the color in my life line."

She smiled and glanced to Cole, who nodded and grinned. "That was really sweet."

"What if he…" Fear of rejection filtered into her bloodstream and her heart pierced in pain. "Charly, have you ever truly seen the way he looks at you?"

She stared up at Cole and blinked. "I never thought about it. Okay, I'll talk to him." She stepped away from Cole and turned to the door when it opened. Out of instinct, she jumped back and both guys hurried forward.

"I didn't mean to startle you," the man told her with a grimace. "I was told that this gallery was taking the mail for Joey Sinn?"

She nodded.

"Yes, you can drop it off here," Cole told him coolly. Neither he nor Jason moved from near Charly.

"Fantastic, let me go grab it." He returned moments later with a large bin and smiled. "Where should I put it?"

"On the floor is fine," Jason answered.

The mailman nodded and set it down. "I'll grab the rest." He hurried out the door and walked in with a large bag. He set it down as well. "Crazy artist. Held her mail for pickup and she never got it. They were starting to go crazy."

"Well, thank you, I'll make sure the post office gets the box and bag back."

He laughed. "You mean bags. I have another two in the truck. Let me go get them." He turned and left again.

Charly was stunned. "Oh my God!" She moved closer. "This is crazy."

"That is a lot of mail," Jason agreed, and grabbed a black envelope off the top. "These envelopes are not ones I want you opening." Her heart sank.

"No, Jason and I can pull them. I know a few beat cops that can read them," Cole told her calmly.

The mailman walked in, and behind him Jacque came in carrying the other bag. "I come bearing mail instead of food," Jacque told her. I see you're already popular." He glanced to the other mail.

The mailman shook his head at Jacque, then grimaced. "I hate to say this, but I need to empty the bags and take them with me." He dumped the contents over the floor scattering letters, then proceeded to empty the other two bags. Washing her floor with an ocean of envelopes, neither she nor the three men spoke. They were stunned. "Have a nice day, and thanks for helping us out." He turned and walked out the door.

"Talk about a disgruntled mail employee." Cole looked down to the floor. "Jason, Jacque, can you guys start helping me weed the black envelopes out?"

"More from the psycho bastard?" Jacque asked, and bent down, picking up black envelopes. There had to be at least fifty of them.

The door opened again and Ruth Valiant walked in. She glanced at the floor and around the gallery. "Oh good, Charly, you're here. I need a word with you."

Charly was sick to her stomach. "Now isn't a good time, Ruth."

Ruth looked to the wall where the empty canvas hung. She looked back to Charly. "No fabulous painting from the elusive Joey Sinn?"

"No, now go be thankful somewhere else. Know that Satan isn't here. I will, however, let him know you stopped by."

Her brows lifted. "You hate me."

Pulling her bottom lip between her teeth, she fought the urge to cry. "I don't hate." She glanced up at the ceiling to the amazing lights and then back to Ethan's mother. "As tempting as it is, not even you."

She glanced to the wall, then to the floor before resting her eyes again on Charly. "Why haven't you painted?"

"You'll be pleased to know that I can't."

Ruth stepped closer to the blank canvas. "It survived the fire almost unmarked. You should paint what's in your heart."

"I can't."

Turning, Charly looked to Ruth as she studied the canvas. "What happened here?" She pointed to where the canvas had dipped from Charly's back while Ethan had made love to her.

"Never mind. You're the last person I want to tell."

Her brows lifted again and she pursed her lips. "Then don't tell anyone. Show them. I know who you are, Charly."

"You sound like my stalker."

"No, and I didn't set the fire to the place. You can ask Cole; I've been cleared."

Charly closed her eyes and refused to open them. If she kept her lashes tightly together, maybe the tears wouldn't fall. Hot tears escaped and descended her cheeks. She opened her eyes. "I can't, and frankly, if I ever paint anything again, it'll be a miracle."

"You truly loved him."

*Wow, the woman has a clue. It only took my heart shattering for that revelation.* "I think you should go."

"Charly—"

"Mrs. Valiant, I think you should go," Cole told her as Charly buried her face in her hands.

"Remember what I said, Charly," she called.

Charly spun on her heel and lifted her head. "That's the problem, Ruth. I have a constant playback of everything you've ever said." Her voice broke and a sob escaped her. Ethan's mother walked out and Charly sunk to the floor. Her knees rested on the envelopes, and with tear-filled eyes, she took a handful. "I quit, I'm done. I'm just going to tell the world the truth." All three guys sighed, and as her heart ached, she cried.

Ethan stared out the window of the fire station office upstairs above the garage. Over the last week, he'd done it a lot. It wasn't like there was anything happening outside. It was all happening on the inside. The inside of his body and soul, that is. Nothing seemed right these days. He was miserable and he knew it, the guys he worked with knew it, and even Cole knew it. Still, Ethan had denied it. Not only to those around him, but for the most part, to himself. Until now. He tried to inhale a breath, but the same constriction across his chest settled over him. It was impossible to fill his lungs with air. Closing his eyes, he tried not to think of the cause of it.

Charly.

She had turned his world upside down.

The way she talked and laughed, the way her voice came across like a gentle caress. Ethan felt devoid, his soul was gone, and the thing was, he couldn't blame her. He had given it to her so willingly. How did you walk away from the person holding your soul? He wasn't sure, but apparently knew the answer since he'd done it without a second thought.

He had fallen for her hard and fast and never thought twice about it. He had thought of nothing but her. In the week and two days of not speaking to her, it hadn't changed.

She had taken the courage and strength to be as honest as she dared. She sighed. He thought he'd heard her, but looking back, he hadn't been listening. The shock of the reality that her life was something stranger than fiction was a tough concept to swallow. The thing was, she had lied, and in doing so, had held so much back.

He could have protected her. He could've worked with Cole and the police. Ethan opened his eyes.

*She never would have let me. She's too independent. Does the woman not know how to trust?*

Not only had he let her down, he had let himself down. He glanced to the phone. He could call her and tell her he was wrong. Then again, she had the number; she could have called and hadn't. He tried to pretend that he'd never felt anything. He had to forget her. How could he? Charly Jamieson AKA Joey Sinn was unforgettable.

Unforgettable as the warmth of the early dawn's light while rising through the pink and blue, revealing what indigo is. She had revealed so much of who he was to himself. A self-discovery process that he was beginning to think had just cost him not only his heart, but also his happiness. Ethan didn't know how to fix this and believed it was one of those things beyond repair.

Charly was everything that the image of Joey Sinn captured. Only she didn't see that. She was the passionate artist with sex appeal. She saw herself as the single mom in ripped jeans with paint in her hair and a small addiction to everything fattening. She was far from fat. Curvy, beautiful, and from what he knew, in love with him. Probably not now; that loss pierced his heart.

Trying to inhale another deep breath, he failed again, and released the air from his lungs in a heavy sigh. This was not getting him anywhere. Turning away from the window, he banished all thoughts of the woman he'd loved and still did. He headed to his desk and threw his body into the plush chair.

A knock came on his door and he sighed, turning his head to a painting that Leigh had made him. His heart tightened. "Come in."

The door opened and Jacque, the crazy but amazing chef walked in. Ethan was surprised. He was even more surprised to see he was with Jason and Cole.

"What are you guys doing here?" He was happy to see them, but they were all a reminder of Charly.

*Charly. What if something is wrong?*

"We just wanted to swing by and see how you are," Cole told him, and glanced to Leigh's painting. His eyes rested on him again.

"Are Leigh and Charly okay?" *Please tell me they are okay.*

"Actually, Leigh is good, but Charly is a wreck. She almost cancelled the gallery opening after the fire." Jason's gaze narrowed on him.

"She is in love with you, Ethan."

He removed his attention from Jason and turned to Cole. "She lives a lie; she and my mom will never get along. I was stupid to think that when she told me that she loved me, she meant it."

"No," his friend started. "She kept her paint name a secret. Joey Sinn is gaining quite a following and her stalker is a crazy, obsessed fan. It's no wonder everything was hushed about it. Hell, she even has a card company coming out with sexy, romantic cards. The world loves her."

"We thought you might too." Jacque sounded disappointed.

Ethan stared at the man. "I tried to set things right with her. I even bought her flowers, and when I got to her house early in the morning, I watched you walk out of her house and hug her."

"She cried her heart out, heartbroken. I did what any man like me would do. I baked for her and made supper for her, Leigh, and Jenna."

Ethan frowned. "You baked and cooked for her?" He bounced his look over the three men in front of him.

"You do realize she has a killer sweet tooth, right?" Jason snorted. "How she maintains that body is beyond me."

"I'm aware of her addiction to sweets." His heart ached and he looked back to Jacque. "I thought something different."

Jacque glanced nervously at Jason and Cole, then looked back at Ethan. "I have Ambrose and she is the only pussy for me." He smiled and tossed his head. His dark eyes danced.

"No way," Jason breathed in disbelief.

Ethan and Cole exchanged a stunned look. Ethan glanced back over at Jacque. His lips parted in surprise at this revelation and interesting development.

*The only pussy...*

He debated a moment. "So, you prefer the strudel as opposed to the soufflé?"

"Oui, I do." He crossed his arms across his chest. "You no tell?"

Ethan smiled. "We won't tell."

"Rumor is the gardener does too, prefer the strudel that is." Jason snickered. "Maybe something for you to keep in mind."

Jacque uncrossed his arms and shoved a hand through his hair. "Maybe."

"Ethan." Cole sighed. "She loves you, man, and her muse is almost dead. She had lost it, then found it, then came up with the most brilliant stuff, but when you walked away, she lost it again."

"I just don't see it working, and I doubt now she'll even want me."

"What if we proved to you that wasn't the case?" Jason asked. "After all, do you really think we would waste our time to come here and see you feel sorry for yourself if we thought she didn't?"

"We want to show you something." Cole motioned to the door.

"What?"

"Get your ass up and just follow us," Jason groaned.

He got up out of the chair and followed the guys out of the office. They led him down through the station and across the street to the gallery. Ethan's back stiffened.

"Relax, she's not here." Cole unlocked the door and opened it. "After you."

Nodding, Ethan stepped through the doors. It smelled fresh with paint and a trace of her perfume. What remained of his heart mourned her not being there. The other guys entered as he scanned the floor covered with envelopes. He looked to them. "What happened in here? What are all these?"

"Fan mail for the ever popular Joey Sinn," Jason told him, and shook his head. "With the new greeting cards with her prints and galleries all over demanding her work because they can't keep it in stock, she has quite the following."

He picked up a handful of envelopes. One of them was damp. "Why are some of them wet?" He was confused.

"That would be where she broke down and cried most likely, before Liz took her home." Jason looked to Cole and then back at Ethan. "We all watched her break down. She's going to reveal her identity tomorrow, not live a lie."

Ethan stared at the multicolored envelopes in his hand. He glanced to the floor. "She won't have a moment's peace. Instead of one crazy fan, she'll have more. She can't do that."

"We know, but she won't listen," Jacque told him. "No one sends me mail over my food."

"Why would she reveal her identity?"

"She loves you," Jason whispered as the four of them stood and stared at the scattered mess of fan mail.

Cole stared at him. "She doesn't want to live the lie. She loves you."

*What have I done?*

"I love her too." He had more than blown it with her. His stubbornness had cost him everything that mattered. That everything being Charly.

His head reeled and his chest constricted so tight that that he couldn't take in air or push a breath out. He was going to die. Then again, since she had walked away, he'd been dying. He turned and stepped over to the large gallery window.

Ethan's body was weak. He leaned his arm against the glass and stared out. What he was actually doing was staring at his reflection in the glass. The image of him in the window glared deep within him. It knew the truth and knew only he could fix this with Charly. Ethan knew he probably couldn't, but he had to try. Despite the other three guys' eyes on him, he closed his eyes and started to pray. He poured his heart out and asked for help. He opened his eyes and looked to the guys. "Tell me one of you has a plan."

The three men exchanged unreadable expressions. "No, not really," Jason admitted. "However, tomorrow night is the gallery opening, so we could maybe come up with one while we pick up this mail."

Ethan looked to the wall. The canvas was blank. What shards remained of his heart stopped beating. "Isn't that picture supposed to be done for tomorrow?"

"No muse, no painting."

Ethan glanced to Jacque, then back to the canvas. He'd made love to her against it. The mark from her back still marred the canvas as the loss of her in his life marred his soul. "I need air." He dropped the envelopes and walked out of the gallery. He sucked in the cool breeze. He couldn't breathe, why would he need air? What he really needed was Charly.

Charly woke to see the moon still casting a glow over the night sky. She groaned and glanced at the clock. Apparently, she had only been asleep a couple of hours. It was two in the morning and the canvas in the gallery was still blank. She didn't feel like painting, and tonight her client was going to want the painting. The canvas was untouched. It was symbolic. He had left an imprint on her heart and soul too.

She felt icky, remembering the pint of Rocky Road she had consumed. Not only had she consumed countless calories, she was still miserable and missed Ethan. She longed to call him and explain she wasn't going to live a lie anymore. She was going to tell the world, at least those at the gallery tonight, that she was Joey Sinn. The plain woman with a stubborn eight-year-old and ripped jeans was the never seen, mysteriously sexy, essence of sensual, always sultry Joey Sinn. There was a good chance no one would believe it. She could always hope.

Readjusting, she sat in bed, thinking of the night she'd had and all the work she had done at the gallery. She thought of the heartache she still endured and the empty canvas. Though nauseated and sad to the depths of her soul, not to mention sleep deprived, she felt restless. More than restless, she needed to burn energy. Where was this coming from? She wasn't sure, but she currently blamed the sugar in the ice cream.

Struggling with the weight settling over her chest, she decided she wasn't going to shed another tear over a man. Charly knew that wasn't true or possible, since her body hurt. She and Ethan hadn't known each other long, but she swore to her soul he was the one. Everything now was completely wrong. Maybe it was because the time with Ethan had been so right. Maybe she was wrong. She didn't want to be, but maybe he wasn't the one. If he was, shouldn't he be hurting too? Shouldn't he be missing her? Shouldn't he have called to try and work things out? Then again, she hadn't called him either. She was too afraid it would just make things worse.

Charly buried her head in her hands and the headache started. This wasn't going to happen. The heartache and nausea were enough. She didn't need the throbbing headache too as a reminder that she was as unhappy professionally as she was romantically.

She kicked the heavy feather duvet off her, and it crinkled and rustled from the Egyptian cotton that encased it. She pulled her white Lycra undershirt down so it came above the navel ring she now was able to put in her thinner, and somewhat flat, tanned stomach. She was everything she had wanted to be. Then why was she so miserable?

*Ethan. It's all about Ethan,* the devil on her shoulder reminded. *You lied to him and can't stand his mother,* the angel snapped in addition. It wasn't like there was a shortage of amusement or men in her life, but only one she wanted to be amused by. She fought the new wave of ache that thoughts of Ethan always caused and swallowed back the urge to cry. Grabbing the gray sweats off the floor, she pulled them on, then the hoodie that matched. She straightened the silver heart necklace on the black leather woven chain around her neck and stomped over to the dresser. She shook her head and noted silently that she had worked more hours than had been sane. That's all she did these days and it couldn't go on like this. She pulled on her socks and then the white leather runners.

Charly needed a change of pace. She needed something that would not remind her every time she moved, blinked, or struggled to breathe of Ethan. Maybe she should go out and have some fling with some guy that meant nothing. The devil on her shoulder jumped and screamed with joy. Unfortunately, the angel on the other side sat down and started the lecture, in a not so heavenly voice, that there was no getting over Ethan. Like she needed the reminder.

"Stupidity!" she grumbled, and headed to her bedroom door. The thing was, she wasn't sure if she was referring to the annoying devil on her shoulder, the man that had shattered her heart into a thousand pieces, or herself for not just being honest with Ethan in the first place then letting his mother come between them. Charly grunted and walked down the stairs then headed to the front door. She peered in the living room where Jenna was asleep on her sofa.

Charly opened the door. The cool night air assaulted her and forced its chilly presence down her throat into her lungs. Her body responded by a nudge of adrenaline, which was now replacing the blood in her veins. She needed to clear her mind and cleanse her soul. Closing the door quietly behind her, she stretched her muscles and stepped off the small porch. The rubber of her shoes hit the pavement of the walk and she took in her first breath, then pushed her left runner down hard and switched to a run.

She focused on the steady sound of her runners hitting the pavement and likened it to the sound of a broom on a hardwood floor. Her mind brought up thoughts about the gallery and the things wrong with it. She thought of the men in her life and her lips twitched into a smile. Her heart beat faster. She loved them all, but there was only one man she could admit she was in love with. Charly could admit it now with a little less pain than before she had left the house.

Deep breaths pushed her lungs into a steady rhythm that accompanied the sound of her movement. She thought and debated over the last few weeks of her life. At times, her pace picked up with the angry thoughts and slowed when her mind tormented her with the sweet things she and Ethan had shared. Every conversation and memory rose to the surface.

They were resurrecting themselves like lost spirits, ghosts from graves that pushed forward so as to not be forgotten. She felt the slow burn in her leg muscles and enjoyed the pain. The burn of a good workout had always helped. It was the familiar burn of muscles having taxed themselves to new extremes that reconnected her with the woman she had been, a time when she had been younger and stronger. Maybe she wasn't so weak now.

Charly slowed her pace and walked. Coming to the neighborhood playground, surrounded by the large and overly ostentatious homes, she thought of Jenna and the words she had spoken one day on the phone.

"You have done nothing but overcome and achieve. You've never missed your mark. I think you can do anything you set your mind to."

She continued to walk and placed her hands on her hips. She breathed deep and thought of her friends who had been there during the darkest hours with the crazed fan. She was somewhat safe now and had built a life for herself and Leigh. Though, being out by herself at night maybe wasn't truly brilliant with the crazed fan lurking. She had done everything she had ever set out to do. If she could do all that, then maybe there was more she could do.

A cool wind rose up and moved some red tendrils that had escaped her ponytail. "Have faith," it whispered as it died down as quickly as it had risen up.

She blinked and glanced up at the sky. "I can do that," she told the heavens, the ears that listened to prayers and desires in hearts. Suddenly, she knew beyond all what she had to do.

She had to go to the gallery and paint that picture, then somehow, someway had to get Ethan back. Charly started to pick up pace and eventually fell into a run again, heading for home. Getting Ethan to even listen to her was going to be tough. Convincing him to give their relationship a second chance was impossible, but if Charly had done one thing really well in her life, it was prove that nothing was impossible.

## Chapter Twelve

Ethan walked along the beach for what felt like miles. He listened to the sound of the water meet the shore and tried to let it soothe the ache in his heart and soul, tried to put distance between the gallery and the words that the three guys had told him. He tried to banish the images of all the fan mail. There had been black envelopes in the pile. Ethan thought of all the black envelopes Charly had received and hated them. He had no clue how many the guys had already picked up.

He loved his mom, but he was in love with Charly. Just thinking of her ached him, and the distance with his mother wasn't pleasant. He knew his mother was only trying to watch out for him. That was fine in the past, but this time, he was sure she had been wrong. He knew she was. Charly had lied, and though it wasn't right, she had been preserving her safety and that of Leigh's. He was tired and his whole body hurt. Actually, he felt broken. Ethan wanted to cry and struggled not to give in. She had done something that usually only memories of his father caused. He hadn't realized that, no longer a boy and now a man, it was possible to hurt this deeply or badly.

Stopping, he turned to stare out at the water, and the cool breeze chilled his already frozen body. The view of the ocean offered little comfort, despite the fact it was an amazing scene. He knew Charly would love this, then no doubt spend a good twenty minutes sketching it in loving detail so she could paint it later. His body betrayed him and a tear formed on his lashes. Ethan quickly wiped it away and demanded his body not to allow this. He stepped to a large group of rocks and climbed on them so he could face the water. The offshore wind cooled him.

He thought long and hard on how he felt and realized that Charly had brought so much to his life. She and Leigh completed it. Hell, she would even have gotten along with his mom, but their ideas about what was right clashed. He could get past the fact she had lied, and it hadn't bothered him when he'd first found out; it shouldn't bother him now. She was independent. He knew it, and it was one of the things he loved about her. Ethan had seen how crazy the stalker was. If she revealed her identity, she could end up with more of them. Charly had been devastated over the gallery, yet her fiery and stubborn demeanor had taken over. She had prevailed, and now tomorrow, the gallery was going to be opening, without him. Her enthusiasm had sparked him, the way she saw beauty and good in everything.

She had loved him, truly loved him, and it was only right by the way he felt about her.

Ethan loved her too and wasn't sure when he had started. He wondered if it was from the moment he first saw her—positive he'd lost his heart that moment. It had been love at first sight and a little bit of lust. She'd stolen his breath and stopped his heart. Who knew that such emotions really existed? He did now.

Charly inspired, dared, and most of all, dreamed. The woman was all he could have wanted and then some. She had been given to him as a gift and he had let her walk away without a chance to explain. He was never going to recover from that if he didn't win her back. She had been the answer to a prayer from his heart's hidden corners. In return, he hadn't listened. He knew that because he was sitting there now, hurting as if he had just suffered a mortal blow.

Shaking his head, he tried to banish the picture of Charly from his mind, so pretty, so willing to be his. How could he forget laughter that played in his head like a favorite song? How could he forget the soft, shy words of a woman falling for him when he woke every morning just to hear them? How could he banish the prettiest thing he had ever seen from a mind that had seen so much ugliness? Ethan would never forget these things, just as he knew he would never forget her.

He reached into his pocket and pulled out his cell phone, then dialed the number. He had to talk to his mother. He had to fix this, but he was going to need the woman's help and her blessing.

"Hello?" his mother greeted from the other end.

He wasn't going to take no for an answer. "Hi, Mom. Do you have a second? I need to ask you something."

"Ethan, it's almost one o'clock in the morning. Is everything okay? You're not hurt, are you?"

He felt a light mist touch his face as the wind changed direction. "Actually, Mom, I'm hurt really badly, but not in the way that you might think."

"What's the matter?"

He debated then went for honesty. "I've made the worst mistake of my life."

"Everyone says that. You're a good man, Ethan. I'm sure whatever you've done can't be that bad. If it's causing you this much hurt then you need to fix it."

"What if it seemed impossible to fix?"

His mother sighed. "That's where faith comes in."

Ethan shivered, hesitated, and pondered his next question. He decided to ask it anyway. "What if you were afraid of hurting someone else if you tried to mend the first problem?"

A weighted sigh came through the cell phone. "Ethan, is this about Charly?"

He stared at the large wave as it rolled in and crashed against the shore. "What if I said it was?"

"Then I would say we have a lot to talk about."

His heart tightened and he closed his eyes. That's what he'd been afraid of. "Yes, it's about Charly."

There was a long stretch of silence. "Well, then I guess that only leaves one question now."

Ethan opened his eyes and exhaled slowly. "Which is?"

"Are you going to say your thing, or will you let me go first?" She cleared her throat. "There are a few things I have to say about that girl."

Ethan cringed. He could only bet there were.

Charly took a step back and stared at the canvas in front of her. It was the most personal piece she had ever done in her life. However, it reflected both her and Joey Sinn and captured the heat, lust, and passion Ethan had sparked. She had brought color to the gray surface and thought of all the laughter, happiness, and love that he'd given her. She just had to figure out a way to talk to him. Charly glanced out the window and still didn't see his car in the parking lot at the fire station. She furrowed her brows slightly. He was supposed to go back on duty today and would have had his days off already. Maybe he'd had a late night.

The thought of him in another woman's arms rolled her stomach with nausea. She closed her eyes and hung her head as the new bells that Cole and Jason had put up jingled. Charly lifted her head as Liz walked in with Jason and Cole. Cole held a tray of coffees and the smell was divine. "What are you guys doing here?"

Liz rolled her eyes. "We got a panicked call from Jenna saying that you didn't come home last night and had left a note saying that you were going to the gallery. So, she is with Leigh, we swung by Jacque's, who insisted you would be famished, and you know how he is about feeding your hunger."

"The man still wants to get naked for you," Cole laughed.

"So does the gardener, as I recall," Jason chuckled, grabbing one of the coffees and turning to Charly. Lifting a bag in his hand, Jason glanced behind her to the wall. The bag lowered, as did the hand with the coffee. Charly took the cup as Jason's mouth dropped open. "Oh my God!"

Cole and Liz stared at the wall in complete awe. Liz walked closer to the no longer empty canvas as Cole stepped to the counter and set the tray with the coffees down. He then walked slowly away until he stood next to Liz.

They all studied the picture, but nobody spoke.

Silence may be golden, but this wasn't a good sign. *This is very bad. You shouldn't have put so much of yourself into it.* The angel pouted. *Oh! Shut up!* the devil barked at the angel.

"Could one of you please say something?" Charly pleaded, then took a sip of her much needed coffee. Her three friends turned, glanced at each other, and then at her. Still, they said nothing. "Okay, you don't like it."

Liz gasped. "Honey, it's amazing."

Blinking, she was surprised. "Really?"

"Do I even want to know what you're going to make off this?" Cole asked, turning back to the painting on the wall. "Charly, it's unbelievable." He looked back at her and grinned. "It's completely you."

"Personally, I think the customer is going to love it," Jason agreed as the bell jingled again. Charly turned.

It was Ruth Valiant. There were days when there was a silver lining to the clouds. There were other days where the rain clouds that often hung over the characters in the Peanuts cartoon blocked any chance of a silver lining from the sky. Today, that Snoopy rain cloud had just threatened to ruin her morning. Sighing, Charly remembered the conversation yesterday. "Good morning, Ruth."

Ruth smiled and stepped closer to her. She sipped her coffee and waited for Ruth to comment as well as notice the painting on the wall. "You look much better today, Charly." Her gaze turned to the painting and she smiled. "I see that it is no longer a blank canvas." She walked closer to the art.

Shooting a blanching look to her three friends, they looked just as apprehensive as she did. She focused her attention on Ethan's mother and held her breath. "I know you are dying to comment," Charly stated, having to break the silence stretching on for too long.

Turning, Ruth smiled. "I can't believe you took my advice."

*I can't believe you know I had sex with your son against it.* "I did."

Ruth nodded, then darted another glance back to the picture before she stepped toward Charly. "I see both the passionate artist in you and the light you bring to my son. More so, I see how he inspires you."

*After that painting, so does the rest of the world.* "Well, it's kind of a moot point now."

Ruth furrowed her brows. "Do you love him?"

"Yes." The single word fell off her tongue in a pain-covered whisper.

"I think you and I need to talk."

"About what? Ethan is no longer an issue." She didn't mean to sound bitter and felt guilty over the fact she did. Not a fantastic sensation, that was for sure. "Ruth, I was just going to go

254

home and get ready. I have to talk to the caterer and I would like to see Leigh before she goes to Mrs. Newman's tonight."

"Actually, I was going to borrow your truck to get the buffet tables with Jacque," Jason told her from behind.

Turning, she nodded. "Fine, then you can give me a ride home and you can take the truck."

"Well, I'm here and I was going to see Mrs. Newman. I'll give you a ride home, Charly. That way, we can have that talk," Ruth said.

*I'm screwed either way. Either I listen to her, or I suffer the wrath of being rude to her yet again.*

Swallowing hard, Charly nodded. "That would be very nice of you." She glanced quickly to her friends. Liz looked skeptical, Cole was nodding, and Jason looked damn unsure. She sighed and turned back to Ruth. "I just have to clean up."

"Go, I'll make sure that your brushes are clean," Liz assured.

*So much for delay and procrastination.*

She smiled at her friends. "Thanks. Cole, you'll make sure everything gets locked up?" He nodded. "I'll see you guys tonight." She inhaled deeply and took a heavy sip of her coffee, allowing it to burn her tongue. "I guess I'm ready."

*Okay, not really ready, but there is no chance I can squeeze in a root canal, which would equal the same agony. I might as well suck it up and be polite.*

"Wonderful, see you all tonight." Mrs. Valiant waved and headed to the door.

*See them tonight? What the hell?*

Charly followed and tossed a glance back to her friends with a pleading look, then walked outside. The air was cool and she looked to the mother of the man she loved. She came to a stop on the sidewalk. "Ruth, we aren't going to fight, are we? Honestly, I don't think my nerves or my heart could take it."

"I don't think we are, Charly. I know things have been rough. I want to try and put some of our differences aside."

She nodded as the woman hurried around to the driver side of a burgundy BMW. "This is your car?"

She smiled. "Yes, I always wanted a nice car and Ethan bought it for me. He's a good son and a great man, Charly."

"I know."

The other woman studied her from over the roof of the vehicle. "I wonder if you also know he is in love with you."

Closing her eyes, she willed herself not to cry. Again, it was futile. Tears stung her eyes and water filled them. She opened them and reached for the car door. "Let's have this talk in the car?" Charly opened the passenger door and climbed in. Her nerves ran high and her palms started to sweat. She glanced over to Ruth and smiled.

Ruth returned the gesture and started the car. "You never answered me. Do you know that Ethan loves you?"

"I did," she admitted, doing up her seatbelt. "I don't think it matters now, though. We officially aren't speaking to each other."

*Don't hurt and don't cry.* She brushed the few tears away that had attacked before getting in the car.

"Have you thought of trying to talk to him?"

"Yes, but I won't cause problems between you and your son." She sipped her coffee to avoid adding anything to that.

Ruth turned onto the freeway and sighed. "Actually, I think you and Ethan not speaking is causing problems between me and my son."

*Typical, I can't win for losing.*

"I'm sorry." What else could she say? Nothing. Anything else would reveal the hurt consuming her.

"I know you are a successful gallery owner. At least you were in New York. Ethan told me. I know your work and overnight success as Joey Sinn wasn't what you were expecting."

"I never told Ethan that."

"It wasn't Ethan that told me. I heard it from Mrs. Newman."

*So much for the church lady keeping a secret.*

"Everyone adores you. Your work as Joey Sinn depicts nakedness, passion, and usually sex."

*Okay, time to take my chance and jump out of the moving car.* "I understand that. No offense, I know what I paint."

"Since you're Joey Sinn, I can only assume that you will be continuing to carry the work in the gallery. You have a huge following." She turned off the ramp toward the upscale residential area where Charly lived.

"Yes, I'm still carrying the artwork of Joey Sinn, and soon everyone will know that I'm her. I'm announcing it tonight at the gallery opening. Mrs. Newman had the hat story and I decided maybe it's for the best."

Ruth sighed. "I wish you wouldn't; you were doing fine." They pulled through the guard gate onto the elusive street where her house was.

"No, I wasn't doing fine." She glanced as they came to a stop in front of her house. She turned in the seat and stared at the woman next to her. "I'm so sorry, Mrs. Valiant. We don't get along and we have a totally different outlook on things. I won't put Ethan through that. I know you raised him by yourself. I won't."

"Charly—"

"I lost the man that not only inspired me, but gave me a new outlook on things. I loved your son, I still do, and I most likely always will." She undid her seatbelt. "Thanks for the ride."

Smiling weakly, Ruth nodded. "You're welcome. Why don't you try talking to Ethan?"

"Ethan knows where to find me and he hasn't. Thanks again." She opened the car door and climbed out, shutting the door behind her. Charly didn't look back. Hell, she tried to forget the last ten minutes of her life. She failed miserably, and as she unlocked her front door, she debated about calling Ethan, but wasn't sure what to say.

She sighed and went to shut her door when Jacque came over. "I need to slip my quiche in your oven."

She lifted her brows. "Pardon?"

He smiled wickedly and held up a cookie sheet with mini quiches on it. "The appetizers for tonight."

She nodded and stepped back so he could walk in. "The kitchen is all yours."

Grinning, he walked into the kitchen and she shut the door. Leigh's fast steps were on the stairs and flew around the corner. "Mommy!" She wrapped her arms around Charly. Charly was careful that the coffee didn't escape out of the white plastic lid and on the excited eight-year-old.

"Hi, honey, where is Aunty Jenna?"

Jenna's footsteps come down the stairs. "I'm here; we were just getting her stuff ready for Mrs. Newman's."

Nodding, Charly stroked Leigh's hair. "You're going to be good for Mrs. Newman, right?"

"She says it's going to be a sleepover and that we're going to have fun."

Charly passed Jenna her cup, then bent down to her daughter. "You know I love you?"

"Yep, and you are going to be a star." Her daughter wrapped her arms around her neck. "I'm going to finish packing." She tore off around the corner and sped up the stairs before Charly even straightened out.

Jenna passed her the coffee back as Jacque walked over to her. "How was the ride from Ethan's mom?" She lifted her brows. "Liz called and warned me."

Sighing, she glanced at Jacque, then back to Jenna. "It was more than interesting. You will never believe what was said."

Jacque laughed. "Try us, *chérie*."


Ethan walked in the door of the gallery to see Cole and Jason standing by the counter talking. There was no sign of Charly. She was most likely in the back office. He glanced down at the large bouquet of roses in his hand.

"Hey, guys."

"Very nice roses. Why do I have a feeling they aren't for Jason or me?" Cole teased lightly.

"No, actually." He took in the room and his gaze fell on the large no longer empty canvas on the wall. "Oh my…" He walked closer to the painting. It was unbelievable. The canvas now turned into a side of a burnt building. Right in the spot that Ethan had pinned her up against to have sex was a couple painted in sexual ecstasy. The man had his back to the audience, and you could tell by the jacket he was wearing that he was a firefighter. The woman's legs wrapped around him and only hints of her hair were revealed. Her legs were bare and her shoes were strappy and seductive. The painting was pure sin. Ironic, it was everything the artist was. He loved Charly and had fallen in love with the Joey Sinn within her.

Ethan blinked and stared at the picture in front of him. It was incredible, despite the fact that it was a little obvious to him, and maybe their friends, that the two lovers having sex were he and Charly. The painting was remarkable. No matter what he tried to tell himself, he knew the truth. "She still loves me."

"Little slow on the uptake, Ethan?" Jason asked and stepped over to him.

He groaned. "I must be as dumb as they come." He glanced back to the painting. "It's unbelievable." He turned and looked around. "Where is she?"

"Getting ready for tonight; it's black tie," Cole reminded him. "Are you going to come?"

"I have the tuxedo. I got it when..." He paused.

*When she was still mine to hold.*

Ethan glanced around the room. Everything looked perfect. He grinned at the guys. "I have to get her to be mine." He hesitated and debated on how honest he should be. "I want her forever and I don't want her to reveal who she is."

"Finally, something smart comes out of my son's mouth," his mother snapped, and Ethan turned to the door where she now stood. "I can't believe you almost let that girl get away."

He blinked as his mother turned to the painting on the wall. He braced himself. "Mom, I know what you're thinking."

"I'm still completely stunned that she took my advice. It's unreal, totally amazing. I can't help but think that is true passion every time I look at it."

"Every time you look at it?" *What the hell?* "When did you see it?"

"This morning, I came by to talk to Charly. She is very upset over our disagreement and even on the ride I gave her back to her place, she just apologized and assured me she is still going to carry the artwork of Joey Sinn."

"Did you say assured you?" Not the words he'd expect to come out of his mother's mouth. He narrowed his gaze on the woman that had raised him single-handedly. "Run that by me again."

"She took my advice yesterday, then melted into a huge pile of fan mail. I felt terrible and told her to paint what was in her heart." His mother waved her hand. "She told me she couldn't, then I asked about the spot in the canvas that was marked and, of course, Charly, the lady she is, told me I was the last person that needed to know."

Oh, his mother knew he had sex with Charly against it. Hell, Cole and Jason now had it confirmed. "You didn't upset her, did you?" Ethan was afraid to ask, but needed to know.

"No, I told her she didn't need to tell anyone. She should show them. It's not like it has your names on it."

*It might as well.*

"I am so pleased to see you inspired her. This is what I was trying to explain to you on the phone this morning when you called me from the beach. I was afraid, Ethan. I was afraid you and Charly would end up in the same mess your father left me in. I didn't understand him. I guess I didn't inspire, but it's not like that with you and Charly. You inspire her."

"Well, I've inspired her to reveal to the world that she is Joey Sinn."

His mother blinked. "She can't do that. You have to stop her."

Ethan looked to Cole and Jason, who shrugged. He looked back to his mother. "Any brilliant idea on how to do that?"

His mother's face lit up. "I think I might. The girl truly loves you." She frowned. "If I help you, will you give me grandchildren? She already has Leigh, so that gives you a bit of a head start now, doesn't it?"

He lifted his brows, stunned. Jason and Cole chuckled. This was unreal. So was the chance he might actually get the girl — both of them.

## Chapter Thirteen

Jenna was gone to Liz's. Leigh had been safely delivered to Mrs. Newman, who had a quick tea with Charly before she sent her on her way so she and Leigh could get on with their play date and slumber party. Jacque had popped over with the last batch of the quiches and now she was finally alone for a few moments. Jacque had assured her that he'd be back for them, and not to worry, he would just let himself in and lock the door behind him.

Charly sat down on the sofa and stared at the picture of Ethan's eyes. She loved his eyes. Hell, she loved him. She glanced around the room, not having a clue what to do with herself until she had to get ready. She could relax and have a glass of wine in a hot bubble bath. Instead, she stared at the painting and missed Ethan.

She was grateful that Leigh wasn't there. Leigh was such a happy child, and right now, happiness was the last thing Charly felt. She closed her eyes, yet she could see the eyes of acrylic still so clearly. They slowly faded to his real ones staring back at her from hundreds of moments they had shared together. She missed him more and her heart tightened. Her lashes opened and she found that the painting was less painful than the images of Ethan she struggled not to remember. "I love you."

She had every reason to be happy. Her gallery was opening, she was successful, and yet, she was empty. Something was completely missing from her and she hated to think that something wasn't a something, but instead, a someone.

Ethan.

She glanced to the phone and wondered if maybe she should try calling him. What would she say? She glanced back up at the picture of the eyes and debated. Sighing, she pulled her bottom lip between her teeth.

"What do you want to hear?" she asked the painting. She knew that, again, she was talking to an inanimate object. "I guess it wouldn't matter what I said as long as I could hear your voice."

Getting up off the sofa, Charly walked over to the end table and reached for the phone. She wanted Ethan there tonight. Even if he didn't want to talk to her, she just wanted to know he was close. Her hand reached for the phone when the doorbell went. It wasn't Jacque. Jacque had a key, as did Cole and Jason in case there was ever an emergency.

Did Leigh forget something? She furrowed her brows, headed to the front door, and unlocked it. Charly pulled it open without looking to see who was there and blinked. She was more than surprised. "Hello, Charly, did you miss me?"

Her heart tightened. Her stomach knotted and a warning bell went off in her head as she stared at the man in front of her. "Stan? What are you doing here?" How in the hell had her former gallery assistant from New York found her? She had told no one but NYPD where she was going.

"I had a hard time finding you. I eventually got it out of one of the galleries that carried Joey Sinn's work." He took off his glasses and put them in his pocket. "I came a long way to see you."

There was something wrong about Stan standing on her front step. "You shouldn't be here, Stan. I have a new life here. Go away."

"I sent you love letters every day, to you and to Joey Sinn both. I know the truth, Charly. I know who you are."

Her blood ran cold and she stumbled slightly back. Her head reeled as she stared at her former assistant. There was something very creepy about this. His words sank into her head and her mind processed. "You sent me all those letters and cards in the black envelopes?"

He smiled and looked pleased with himself. "I wanted to show you how black my soul was since you left. I begged you and pleaded with you. I'm your biggest fan."

Her breathing quickened, as did her heart. Stan, nerdy Stan, who had been so nice, was the stalker. "I think you better go, Stan. I think you should just go back to New York."

He stepped forward. His body shoved her out of the way of the door. "No, Charly, or Joey, whoever the real you is. I'm not going anywhere." He crossed the threshold and smiled. His expression became demonic. Panic started to fill her. What the hell? Never did she think the shy guy was capable of writing so many hateful things to her.

"Stan, I think you need help. One minute you proclaimed love for me, the next you were threatening and scaring me with the things you wrote. Every time I saw a black envelope, I became afraid."

She needed help. Should she scream? Was he carrying a weapon? Oh God, what was she going to do?

"You have no reason to be afraid." The eerie calm of his voice sent the hair raising on the back of her neck.

*Okay, how is terrified, sicko?*

"I'm here now, and everyone and everything is going to be okay."

Stan's large hand shut the door behind him and locked it. He looked unbalanced; he was a complete nutcase. "You're nothing but a bad girl, Charly," he seethed, and closed the distance as she stepped back to avoid his reach. "You ran from me. You left New York. You left me behind. Nobody knew where you were." He stepped closer to her. "I found you. Now why don't you be a bad girl for me and show me what pleasure you can give a man. I know you're Joey Sinn and Joey Sinn is a slut."

"You wish, you lowlife son of a bitch." Fear tickled up her back.

"You think I'm I son of a bitch?" His hand snaked out, and before she could move, grabbed her by the neck. His thumb and forefinger pinched tightly below both her ears. He spun around and the back of her head hit the snow white wall about the same time she realized her feet weren't touching the floor.

"You worked in my gallery in New York, Stan. I paid you well," she choked out.

"But you never gave me affection, did you? You never noticed me as a man. You just painted those perfect specimens, the ones with the rippled chests and the washboard abs." His grip tightened and Charly struggled, kicking him back. She missed and swore that her neck was going to snap.

She thought of Leigh and thought of Ethan. If she survived this, she would go and make things right with him, beg him to listen. She kicked again and made contact with Stan's groin with her knee. He released his hold and she dropped to ground. She fought to take in air and moved out of his reach. Charly grabbed the first thing in her path and threw it at him. The metal can hit him in the head and the lid popped off. Red paint splattered everything.

"You stupid little slut. If I can't have you, no one will. You'll never see another naked man and never paint another picture. That's why I burned your gallery down. You didn't stop; you carried on and rebuilt it." He lunged toward her and she jumped, swiping a handful of paintbrushes. She started throwing them at him as he dove again toward her.

"Stay away from me, you psychotic freak."

He had obviously misjudged and she slipped by him. She moved to the end table and reached for the cordless phone. Charly needed help. He grabbed for the collar of her sweatshirt and missed. Instead, he grabbed her ponytail. She stepped hard in his instep and he groaned in pure rage. He also, though, released his hold on her. She hurried to the cordless phone and grabbed it off the base, moving into the kitchen where at least there were knives.

Her hand shaking with fear, she tried to dial and couldn't from the severe tremble. Stan's footsteps come into the kitchen and she threw the phone at him to slow him down. Not smart. How was she going to get help now? Where did she leave her cell? She turned to the stove and opened the oven door. The smoke alarm went off and she scurried toward the front door.

"You're not going anywhere. You're staying with me. I'm going to be all that you and your inner Joey Sinn the slut will ever need." His hand grabbed her shoulder and he spun her around. She stumbled back and her shoulder blades hit the wall. The alarm drowned out everything save the pounding of her heart in her ears. Stan pulled on the front of her sweatshirt and drew her close to him. Her stomach rolled with fear. "You will love me."

*Oh God, he's going to kiss me.*

She struggled and lost her footing on the tile. She slid and he lowered her to the floor. "Get off me." She shoved him as his body came over hers and pinned her to the ground. "So help me, Stan, get off me." She tried to knee him, but he kept her body restrained. "I'll never love you. You're a sick, stalking bastard. I will, however, put a knife in you." Charly saw his face lower to hers. He had a red welt and a cut that was dripping blood over his temple and down his cheekbone. Most likely, from when she threw the paint can at him.

Too bad it didn't knock him out.

Tears pricked her eyes, and as the water filled them, they started to sting.

"That's it, get angry, be bad." His breath reeked and his dark eyes burned with something that was more than desire. It looked closer to hatred.

There was a thudding sound and a crash. It resembled the dong of a bell. Stan collapsed against her chest and Charly opened her eyes to see Jacque standing there with a frying pan. "*Chérie*, you okay?"

"Get him off me, please," she whispered. Jacque kicked the unconscious Stan off of her. She closed her eyes as heavy footsteps entered the house. Hot tears slid out of her eyes and down across her temples, losing themselves in her hairline.

"What the hell?" Cole's strong voice barked as his footsteps came into the house. Relief washed over her and she heard the sirens in the distance drawing closer. "Someone get this asshole on the floor some smelling salts so I can cuff his ass." Cole's anger radiated and vibrated over every order he barked. Finally, the hotty officer took his job seriously. She couldn't clearly make out what he was saying and slowly tuned him out. Charly still lay on the floor, relieved to be alive, and knew that tomorrow she would feel the altercation in every muscle. There was more movement, the sound of Jason's voice, and then someone at her side.

"Hey, sweetheart," Ethan greeted. She turned to the soft, sexy voice. More tears filled her eyes in relief and she opened them.

Ethan's sexy features softened. She was quite sure that she'd never been happier to see him in her life. "Ethan..." Her voice trailed off and she struggled to get in a sitting position. His strong arms reached out and lifted her. Within seconds, she had crawled onto his lap and his arms wrapped around her.

"Shh," he soothed gently. "You're safe, Charly," he assured. "Forgive me," he whispered as his hand gently stroked her hair. His hold tightened on her and he looked around the room. "Tell me this isn't blood."

"It's paint," Cole answered for her, and hauled Stan up off the floor.

"I have rights. I was assaulted with a frying pan by the naked freak in an apron."

"You have no rights," Cole told him, and shoved him to two other officers. They grabbed Stan roughly and walked him out of the door.

Ethan kissed the top of her head and looked to Jacque. "Why are you in Charly's house naked?"

"I not in all nakedness; I have on an apron. The last of the little quiches are in the oven." His features scrunched. "I didn't like the stranger over here, so I brought a frying pan. No weapon in this apron."

Jason snorted as he crouched down next to Ethan.

Charly glanced to Cole. He had the same stunned look on his face as Jason and Ethan had. "I think we're more concerned about the weapon under the apron."

Chuckling, Jason studied her. "You okay?"

She pulled her lip between her teeth and glanced at Ethan, whose blue eyes rested on her. "I'm not sure."

His hold tightened on her and he drew her close to his chest. "She'll be okay; we'll be okay." Tears flushed down her cheeks and she buried her face in his strong shoulder. "Please don't cry," Ethan's voice soothed. "Charly, please."

Lifting her head, she glanced at him. He shifted her weight and removed an arm from around her, still holding her tight with the other. His hand brushed her tears away. He touched her hair. "You even have paint in your hair." He smiled. "But then, you usually do."

"I tried working things out with your mom."

His lips curved into a lopsided grin. "I know, she told me. She also will kick my ass if I let you slip from my fingers."

Charly wanted to believe him. "Really?"

"I want you. I need you, sweetheart, and I love you."

Raising her shaky arms, she wrapped them around Ethan's neck and hugged him tight. "I love you too." He drew her closer to him again in both arms and held her. "I want to be with you."

A loud sniff filled the room and her attention shifted to Jacque. "I love romantic moments."

Jason chuckled from next to her and she looked to him. "How did you guys get here so fast?"

"We were at the gallery when the call came in, and since we knew there was a good chance it wasn't a fire, we figured something was wrong." Jason smiled and stood. "I think Cole, Jacque, we should go get ready for tonight and let Ethan and Charly have a moment."

"I rescue the little morsels of egg and ham first?" Jacque asked with a lift of his brows.

"Fine." Cole groaned as he stepped over to Charly and helped her out of Ethan's lap. Ethan stood and rested his hand at the small of her back.

She blinked at Cole. "Thank you."

Nodding, he smiled. "Take care of her," he told Ethan. He looked back at her and winked. "Give him hell and we'll see you tonight."

He walked to the door and followed Jason and the naked chef, who was holding a cookie sheet with quiche on it, out of the house. The door shut and she turned to Ethan. There was so much she wanted to say to him and had no clue where to start. "I don't know where to start—"

His arms circled her waist. "Charly, I have only been this terrified once before. The day the windows blew out of the gallery. My world stopped, and I swore if you had been in there my heart would have stopped beating permanently." His eyes scanned her face. "I stared at the wall in my office and I saw Leigh's picture. I couldn't help but think I wanted more of them. I was wrong and I overreacted. Could you ever forgive me?"

Charly's face registered uncertainty. If she didn't forgive him, he'd understand. He had been blind to so much. Ethan again brushed tears from her cheeks. He loved her so much and beyond all.

"I'm sorry my artwork is really racy." She sniffed and slipped her arms around his neck. "I have seen more naked men in my life than—"

"I wouldn't change it, or you. I love Joey Sinn, and I love you, Charly." He brushed escaping tendrils away from her face and smiled. "Out of all the naked men and all the good-looking ones you're surrounded by, it was me."

"It was only ever you, Ethan." She shook her head. "From the moment I first laid eyes on you."

He knew her words were the truth. "I see that now."

She nodded and leaned in closer to him. Slowly, she pressed her full breasts against his chest and her lashes fluttered closed. Ethan closed his eyes as her warm breath caressed his skin and her lips touched his mouth. He groaned slightly, thinking how much he had missed the way their bodies ignited from the slightest touch or caress. He opened his eyes as her lashes opened. Her dark eyes stared at him. "I finished the painting at the gallery for Kendra Kensington."

Nodding, Ethan grinned. "I saw it. I apparently inspired you." He took in her face. It was amazing to hold her again. He had missed her so much; his heart, his soul and his body all had. She truly completed him. "It's as incredible as you are. Glad I could provide you with inspiration."

"I could use your inspiration more." Her voice was low and seductive and his cock stirred at the sultry undertones.

"I think I can help you there."

Her full lips turned into a smile. "Perfect." She closed her eyes and kissed his lips again. This time, they pressed harder. Her tongue slid across his bottom lip and his mouth opened. He had to taste her. He had to explore her mouth. His body hungered for her. It was different, deeper, and above all, it was out of love rather than lust. The ache increased in his pants. He slid his hands down to her firm ass and cupped her flesh. He gently pushed her toward him and her tummy against the hard bulge that begged to be in her.

Her hands ran over his shoulders and down his chest. Ethan tucked his hand under her and took her in his arms. "What are you doing?"

"I'm taking you upstairs, inspiring you, and in the process, showing you what looking at that picture inspired in me." He hurried up the stairs and to the bedroom. He stopped and set her down.

"What's wrong?" Her brows furrowed and Ethan frowned. "You have paint in your hair, on your clothes, and the bed is Egyptian cotton. I don't want to get the sheets dirty since I have every intention of ravishing you in them tonight after the gallery opening."

Charly smiled. "You can ravish me anytime you want in that bed. It's a really big bed without you." She stretched up and lightly kissed his lips. "I love you, Ethan; I really do."

He scanned her face. "I need to go right now, but I want you to promise me that tonight after the gallery opening, you're completely mine."

"I think I've been completely yours since you came barreling in my house and ate my chicken."

Chuckling, Ethan brushed her lips softly with his. He didn't want to leave her, but he wanted to do something before the gallery opening. "I don't want to go, but I'll set the alarm."

Disappointment darkened her features. "I would rather you stayed."

"I know, sweetheart, but my tuxedo isn't here. I promise I'll make this up to you."

She nodded slowly and he grinned. He wrapped his arms tight around her and crushed his lips against hers. His idea was perfect and he loved it more by the moment. He lifted his mouth and smiled. "I'll be back, just worry about looking beautiful and I'll see you tonight."

She blinked a couple times and he walked out of the bedroom. He smiled and had a real good idea how he could make both his mother and Charly very happy.

Charly glanced around the gallery. Everything in Passionate Pleasures looked wonderful. Despite the fact that Stalker Stan had been caught, Cole had insisted there still be an on-duty policeman close by. All her friends were there and several prestigious guests. She took in the room again and sighed. Jacque looked wonderful, making sure that everything with the food and wine stayed perfect. Liz and Jason were talking to a few very sexy men that played for the Angels that were art fanatics. Charly had told Jason to invite them. He had really been there for her over the last few weeks. All her friends had, but as she looked around the room, she still didn't see any sign of Ethan. She had to make her announcement and walked over to where the microphone was.

"Charly, my darling, you are ever the glowing dream," Kendra droned. "I must say that this is another notch up compared to your gallery in New York and I'm thrilled to be one of the elite invited."

"You're the only one from New York invited," Charly corrected. "I knew you wouldn't miss it."

"The picture is amazing." She inched closer to Charly and leaned in. "You truly outdid yourself."

Charly's stomach tightened. "You mean Joey outdid herself?"

Kendra turned and smiled ruefully. "Yes, of course. That painting is worth every penny." She sighed and cast a look around the room before returning her gaze to Charly. "I know your secret, and trust me, it's perfectly safe. I love when a woman wraps herself in mystery. I think that's why I have such a love for you, my dear."

"I almost feel guilty over the price. It's really a lot of money."

"Darling," — she waved her hand — "never sell yourself for less. Trust me, I landed myself four very wealthy — now ex — husbands. The more expensive you are, the more of a luxury you become."

"Thank you, I'm just glad that you like the picture."

"No, I love that picture, and feel the need to throw a dinner party in its honor." She laughed. "Well, let's be frank, I have the need to show it off."

"Well, so much for my mystery. I have to make an announcement and then tend to the other guests. Thank you, Kendra."

"Thank you for the man in uniform in that painting."

Stepping around her, Charly reached for the microphone and sighed. She turned it on and inhaled deep. *I can do this.* "I would like to thank you all for coming this evening and hope you all have a wonderful time. I have received many compliments on the featured painting behind you and the many rave reviews for the artwork of Joey Sinn." She glanced over and saw Jenna and Liz standing with Cole, Jason, and Jacque. They all looked worried. She forced herself to smile broader and continued on, tearing her gaze from her friends. "I would just like to say that, despite the disappointment that some of you have about Joey Sinn not actually being here tonight—"

There was movement to her left and she turned to Ethan. He looked breathtaking. Her face lit up, and for a fleeting moment, she forgot they weren't alone in the room. "You made it."

He reached out his hand and took the microphone gently away from her. He turned it off. "I wouldn't have missed this for the world and I don't want you to tell them. I want to cherish that secret as much as I cherish you."

Her lips parted to speak and he grinned. He flipped on the microphone and turned to her guests. "I'm sorry about that, ladies and gentleman, but we were hoping to have a surprise for you tonight. Unfortunately, Ms. Sinn had to cancel at the last minute. She sends her warmest regards and has invited you to enjoy the painting. Any questions, you can direct to Charly Jamieson. Have a wonderful time and thank you again for coming." He turned off the microphone and focused on her.

"Why did you—"

Ethan placed his finger softly to her lips as the guests resumed conversation and the music filtered in again through the speakers. "I was saving you from yourself."

Ruth Valiant walked over and grinned. "Well, did you get it?" she asked Ethan, who nodded. She turned to Charly. "I've been told that the picture on the wall has been sold."

"Ruth, there are several pictures. To which would you be referring?"

She leaned in then whispered, "The one my son inspired you on."

"You're the inspiration?" Kendra Kensington droned from behind her. She raked her eyes over Ethan and lifted her brows. Sinful thoughts reflected in the features on her face. "Well, you certainly inspire me."

Ethan chuckled and turned to Kendra. "Thank you."

"Well, what did she say?" His mother leaned in closer.

Sighing, he grinned. "I was just about to ask her when you ladies came over."

Charly blinked and quickly darted a glance to the ladies. "Come, Ms. Kensington," Ruth encouraged. "Maybe we can discuss keeping this particular piece in the gallery and maybe put an honorary plaque on it with gold print."

"I'm listening. So, in other words, the whole world will know that I own that marvelous delight. It saves me from having dinner parties."

The women walked away and Charly turned to Ethan. "You were saying?"

"You know there is a good chance that woman might pay you and leave it here. My mother can be very persuasive." His gaze pulled from the older ladies and he reached into his pocket. "I told you when I left your house earlier that I would make it up to you for leaving. So, with that said." He pulled out the black velvet box and opened it. "Will you marry me?"

Charly's hand flew to her mouth. The large diamond winked back at her. She scanned the room and noticed a few people looking. Of course her friends were, and grinning like fools in the process. She glanced back to Ethan. "Absolutely, I'd love to marry you."

Chuckling, he slipped the ring out of the box and slid it on her finger. "I was hoping you would say that. He took her hand in his and stepped closer to her. "I love you."

"I love you too. You made tonight perfect."

His lips brushed against hers. "It is now."

♥

Jacqueline Bloom needs a miracle to save her family's legacy. Who knew life could get worse? Add an obsession over a man in a black and white photo who died in the Korean War with a set of pilot wings given to her by a ghost and her day takes a nosedive. Sometimes though, miracles happen in the strangest places. You sneeze during one earthquake and all of a sudden the year is 1953 and you're mistaken for a car thief.

Captain Hunter Erickson is captivated with the woman whom he thinks stole his car. The more time Hunter spends in the company of Jackie, after an accident that almost costs him his sight and his pilot wings, his curiosity increases and his libido knocks into overdrive. Only, he didn't count on Jackie being from the future, changing his attitude toward marriage or altering his destiny.

Please turn the page
For a preview of

# Irresistible

Available Now

# Chapter One-Irresistible

"It's a little too late in the game to launch into fragrances. This company is struggling. Bloom Cosmetics can't take the financial risk, nor are the resources available for such an expansion. You're not thinking straight, but what else is new?" David glared across the table at her.

Jacqueline Bloom detested her ex-husband's condescending tone. "Odd, you said the same thing when I wanted to divorce you. So far, leaving your ass is my best move yet."

Sharp gasps filled the room. Neil Dickens, sitting next to his son, scowled at her comment. The bad blood between her and David shouldn't surprise her former father–in-law, or the board of directors. Yet, their war often did.

"Don't be a bitch." David's green eyes reminded her of a mean cat ready to strike.

"Why not? I'm good at it." Her heart picked up speed and her temper rose. She tried not to hate, but the man sitting on the other side of the heavy oak table made disliking damn easy. "Screw you David, and your opinion. You and Neil are supposed to act as advisers, but from where I sit, you've done nothing but offer bad advice and prove to be as big a liability to

Bloom Cosmetics as your spending habits were to my bank account."

His eyes glowered and the urge to buy him a scratching post overwhelmed her. "You are in fine form today, Jackie. Tell me —"

"Enough!" Sophia, Jackie's grandmother, silenced not just David, but the entire room with her word and tone. She narrowed her steely blue gaze on the two men. "I think this meeting has covered an adequate amount for today. Everyone, out!"

Jackie should have controlled her anger and animosity, but annoyance fogged her better judgment. She didn't understand why her grandmother kept Neil and David Dickens around, especially knowing how bitter and expensive the separation had been. Then again, her grandfather, Marty Bloom had liked Neil and counted on him. Only now, her grandfather wasn't here. He'd passed away shortly after Jackie had filed for divorce. Her guess, their involvement with the company had gone on so long that her grandmother perceived them as part of the furniture. In which case, time to redecorate.

Rising from her chair, she wished she could go home, soak in a hot tub, have a glass of wine and let the bubbles dissolve the tension currently clenching her shoulders.

Sophia's hand covered hers. "I want *you* to stay."

She nodded her head, lifted her gaze from her grandmother's large diamond dinner ring, withdrew her hand, and walked over to the windows that spanned the length of the wall. Her eyes devoured the Los Angeles skyline as if searching for an answer to a question never asked. The morning sun had struggled to shine, but succumbed to the gray clouds now hanging above and turning the day bleak.

"I know, I lacked professionalism," she confessed, then waited for her grandmother's lecture.

"Your ex-husband is an ass, and his father equally so. I should have gotten rid of them when the divorce became final. I realize my mistake with every argument the two of you insist on getting into. I'm sorry, Jacqueline. I lacked sensitivity."

*Nope, demonstrated poor taste possibly, but who am I to say anything? I should never have married him.*

She kept her sarcastic and bitter thoughts in check and waited for her grandmother to continue.

"Things certainly haven't improved between you and David. I wonder sometimes if they will only get worse." The wheels and leather of the expensive executive chair creaked slightly and her grandmother's footsteps padded softly toward her. Reverting back to the reason for the latest disagreement she grumbled quietly. "I still think we should have launched perfume when we first started, but the fragrance wasn't ready in time. Problems in the early stages delayed things, and then we couldn't afford such a move. Something always came up and we needed the cash."

Jackie shifted her gaze and smiled. "I never realized having a perfume line was an option at one point."

"We would've had to invest extra money and we didn't have the finances. Heavens, child! We started this company on a shoestring. I still don't know how we ever managed to keep the house in Citrus Grove and the one in LA. In an era where having two cars was a luxury, owning two homes was unheard of. Families in the east were more inclined to live that extravagantly, but only the wealthy ones, old money mostly."

Her heart tightened as an invisible heavy weight settled across her chest. She felt the sadness that always washed over her when she thought of her grandfather. "Grandpa told me once he kept the house because he wanted to return to a normal life when the company didn't work out." She shook her head at the irony of that moment. He and her grandmother had come so far, *too* far to fail now.

Jackie tried to smother the pain in her heart and cast a bitter sweet smile at her grandmother. "But after a while, when Bloom Cosmetics was going to survive and flourish, he used the house to think and reflect. He taught me the importance of remembering where you came from."

Sophia's lips thinned in a wry smile. "I'm not as sentimental as your grandfather dear. In fact, I'm thinking of selling the home."

"Since you had new marble tile put in the house here in LA, my guess is you're referring to the one in Citrus Grove."

"I always said you were the smartest of my off spring."

"Maybe that's because you had girls and I'm the only grandchild." Jackie laughed, a halfhearted, sad little chuckle, then suddenly frowned. "But I *love* the house in Citrus Grove!"

"I know." She rolled her eyes and a wry smile curled her lip. "My daughters express no interest in a house in a small town. Then again, they weren't interested in Bloom Cosmetics once they were grown and married. Your mother is happy being a homemaker and Aunt Sue loves to travel. You have my business sense and loved this company before you knew what lipstick was."

She remembered playing on her grandmother's office floor as a child, and later wanting to know how everything worked. By the time she was in her late teens, leaving her mark on the family's legacy became more than ambition, but instead, a part of her soul.

Sophia pursed her lips thoughtfully. "I was in Citrus Grove about a month ago, to pay a maid service and landscapers to keep the place up. I don't find much sense in me keeping the small home."

Jackie's happiest memories were at the little blue two-story with the inviting front porch and the beautiful orange tree shading the large picture window. There she had always felt relaxed when surrounded by the gentle ambiance, like the house and tree were a part of her. But what could she say? When Sophia Bloom made up her mind about something it was game over. Nothing and no one changed her opinion.

"Of course," her grandmother's voice interrupted her momentary pity trip, "if you want the house, I'll give it to you."

The invisible weight on her chest lifted,

and for some crazy reason, the thought of owning that slice of her family's history brought sentimental tears to her eyes. "That little house makes me happy. Thank you."

The older woman nodded almost sadly. At eighty seven she still shouldered the responsibilities of the business like a much younger woman. She suddenly looked tired. Jackie's eyes narrowed. "The money situation with the company is taking a toll on you."

Her grandmother seemed to shake off her slump and replied briskly. "So is having David lurking around and running Bloom Cosmetics into the ground."

She was bitter of course; positive David's poor judgment and bad financial solutions were part of the company's problem.

"You need to take a page out of your grandfather's book and go to Citrus Grove. Hang out at the house, get some sleep and relax. Maybe think on how you'd like to decorate. I don't doubt you will figure something out to help the company."

It was a tempting offer and she needed to get away. Citrus Grove wasn't far, about an hour south of the city, maybe a little longer if an accident delayed traffic.

"I certainly think it'll do you a world of good and will put some distance between you and David."

"So would punting him in the ass and sending him through the air to somewhere over the ocean."

Her grandmother lifted her brows and a sparkle danced in her blue eyes. "You certainly are blessed with my temper. However, remember darling, there are sneakier ways to get back at him. Think on that while you're on vacation. I will see you Monday."

"Gram, today is Tuesday."

"I think you need more than a couple days." Sophia stepped forward and kissed her cheek. "I know how much Bloom Cosmetics means to you. If anyone can get us out of this mess, it will be you." Her arms wrapped around Jackie in a hug.

Jackie's mind raced. The only thing that could save the company at this point would be nothing less than a miracle and, at present, she was fresh out of those.

♥

# Little White Cowboy Lies

Madison Bellini lied…

Madison ran away from her high society family, her money-grubbing fiancé who has sex with anyone but her, and--landed herself a cowboy for good measure. When her car skids on a patch of mud, and she ends up in the river, she finds herself with the sexiest cowboy she could have imagined. What's a girl to do? Lie. If she fakes amnesia then she can't reveal who she is or answer any questions. However, she didn't count on Ty lying too.

Ty Kirkland lied more…

Ty has had enough of women and money trouble. When he finds a woman blowing bubbles in the river and realizes she's an oil heiress with no memory, he decides she might be the answer to both problems at once. Introducing her to family and friends as his fiancée, he thinks he's got it made. Only he wasn't counting on his family adoring her, his libido going into overdrive, or that her amnesia might be faked.

Can Ty and Madison turn their engagement
into a real one despite the lies?

♥

50% of this book's sales will be donated by the author to Susan G. Komen to help find a cure.

## Tickled Pink

*Couples that go to jail together, stay together…at least for one year.*

Interior decorator, Antonia Deluca, had it all figured out. A great career, she's single and carefree, and has awesome friends. Until one of her awesome friend's gives her a gift of *Tickled Pink* and tells her to make a wish. Who believes in such hogwash? Not her, well, maybe…yes. After that moment life takes an unusual twist. Suddenly she's arrested and sentenced to marriage—is that even legal? And her new husband is as uptight as he is gorgeous. One year of dealing with Richard, one annulment and viola, life is back to normal.

Richard Bryson can't believe his bad luck. Unpaid parking tickets lead him to a court of law where his dad is presiding—never good. So, they get off on a technicality, but only as long as he and Toni marry and stay that way for one year. What starts out as a means to an end, soon backfires and somewhere during his sentence Richard falls for his quirky and obsessed with ducks wife. Now he needs to convince Toni they belong together and she really does tickle him pink.

♥

## Rocking Christmas

Single and successful Molly Wright doesn't have time for frivolous things like going home for Christmas. Parcel Post is perfect to send Christmas cards and useless gifts people will never use. However, faster than you can say "stocking stuffer" it's goodbye palm trees, hello Pleasantville. AKA Hell and yes, it's frozen over. How bad could the holidays with her family be? Other than the reindeer in the house and her ex-boyfriend Stryker her brother's best friend, the now famous rock star standing next to the fireplace.

Stryker Blaire has everything money and fame can provide — including writers block for his next album. When his best friend back in the small town he grew up invites him home for the holidays, and with no family of his own, how can Stryker say no? Maybe going back to his roots will provide inspiration for some songs. Wrong, more wrong and pass the eggnog. No one mentioned Molly was going to be there, prettier than he remembered. Forget the eggnog and pass the mistletoe.

Thanks to a matchmaking reindeer, both Stryker and Molly look at their lives and wonder if there is second chance for love when the holiday is over.

## About JT Schultz

My true passion in life is my writing. Corrupted as a child with "Happily Ever After" to the point that now, all my stories have one. Reading great stories and watching movies are also loves, they were the motivation for me to write and explore the "what if..."

Inspiration comes from life, love, stories and sometimes that, which the eye cannot see, but the heart beckons

The road to my writing career has been an interesting one to say the very least. My first published work was a novella and since then, I have gone on to write several other books in a variety of lengths. Check out my bookshelf as my title list will change and grow. Also, my back list will surface, so you can meet or reunite with heroes and heroines of the past.

~Best,

www.jtschultz.com

Made in the USA
Charleston, SC
29 March 2015